POLLYANNA'S CASTLE IN MEXICO

THE EIGHTH GLAD BOOK
(Trade Mark)

POLLYANNA'S

(Trade Mark)

CASTLE IN MEXICO

BY

ELIZABETH BORTON

GROSSET & DUNLAP

Publishers   NEW YORK

To

WILLIAM HARRISON FURLONG,

who opened the gates of Mexico to me, and to the great road from San Antonio to Mexico City, which will open Mexico to many others, and to dear friends in Mexico who made me wish to stay there forever, whatever there may be of good in this little story for young people is affectionately dedicated.

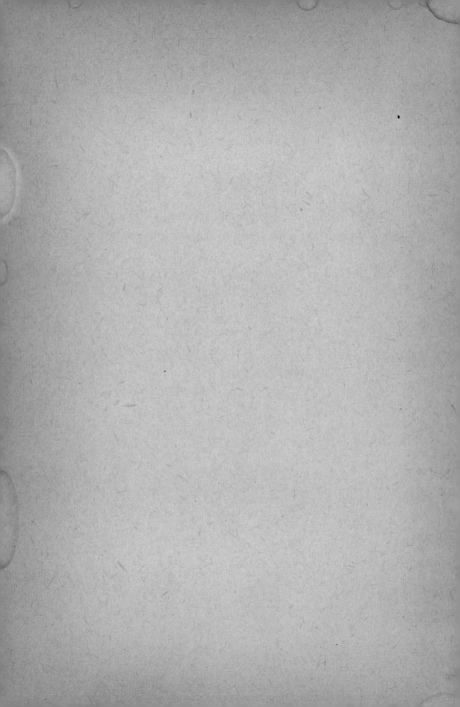

FOREWORD

In taking the Pollyanna characters to Mexico it seems to me that I gave them the very nicest thing it was in my power to bestow. I was happy taking them there, and in writing about what we saw. If there is anything in this little story in any way offensive, or hurtfully inaccurate, about Mexico or the Mexicans, it is entirely unmeant and accidental, for I have only the highest regard and warmest affection for the country and the people.

Elizabeth Borton.

CONTENTS

POLLYANNA'S CASTLE IN MEXICO

CHAPTER I

INTO THE AIR

POLLYANNA took a last look at the packing boxes, suitcases and trunks piled up in the living room of her Hollywood home. She was dressed in a blue tweed suit; to one hand clung Judy in a brown linen frock and to the other Ruth, a globular little person stowed away in a pink print. Junior was tying up the last box.

"Go and find Nancy, Ruth," said Pollyanna, "and tell her that we mustn't delay, because airplanes fly on as strict a schedule as trains or steamers." Small, sturdy Ruth started obediently across the room, but Junior looked up and stopped her.

"Nancy has been crying, Mother," he said. "She is afraid we are all going to be killed."

1

"She is mad at you, too, Mother," said Judy. "She was muttering like everything while she packed our clothes this morning, and she kept saying 'The Lord forgive her if some kind of a bolt falls out of that thingenbob and down they all go.'"

Pollyanna sighed, "Whatever are we going to do with Nancy?" she murmured. "I bought her a ticket to follow us on the train, but now she says she won't go to any heathen country, but she doesn't want to go back to Vermont alone either."

She sat down on one of the trunks, took off her hat, and pressed her hand against her forehead. "I hope I am not doing wrong to fly with you, Darlings," she said a little shakily, and immediately she felt Judy's slim arm around her neck and her soft little cheek pressed against her.

Junior thumped the box he had just finished tying up smartly with his foot and tossed a lock of hair out of his eyes.

"I spent all yesterday with Nancy, Mother," he said, "while you were out saying Goodbye to everybody, and I just can't seem to beat any reason into her. I kept telling her that Dad would be the last person in the world to let you and us do anything dangerous, but she just kept wagging her head and saying 'If the Lord meant for people to get off the earth and fuss around up in the air, he would have put wings on them.' I said to her that the Lord gave people sense enough to invent machines that they could fly in, so that proved he was on our side. And Mama, she grabbed me and shook me something fierce."

Judy put a word in. "I was trying to tell her about Mexico, Mother, but she has the funny idea that it's heathen. I told her that after we got Papa's letter, we had read a lot about Mexico together, and that there was even one city where they had a church for every day in the year, but all she would say was, 'It ain't Christian to be so wasteful.' "

"Did you arrange with Charley Wing about Jiggs?" asked Pollyanna.

"Yes," said Junior. "He said he would take care of him until we got back, but he asked me how long we were going to be away, and I had to tell him we didn't know. Still I don't think Jiggs will forget me, do you?" He was sober, for he loved his dog as boys do, and always have.

"Of course not," said Pollyanna.

"And Charley and I fixed up a plan to exchange pictures," Junior added. "Do you know what we are going to do, Mother? We are not going to take just any old picture and waste a lot of film. We made a bargain that we would take only scenes and people that we just couldn't find any excuse not to

take.   Charley's will be the best, of course, but then
if Dad lets me go with him and the other engineers
down that new road that they are making, I ought
to get some wonderful pictures that maybe not even
any grown-ups have ever taken."

"I am sure you can be a great help to your father,
too," said Pollyanna, and her face brightened at the
thought of rejoining her husband, for though there
had been many short separations in their life since the
work of an engineer calls him many times to places
where a wife cannot follow, the loneliness of being
parted from him had never grown any easier to bear,
even though Pollyanna was the type of woman to
whom her children were a constant and beloved re-
sponsibility and a joy forever.

With the conclusion of his work in California,
Jimmy Pendleton had looked forward to a well-
earned vacation with his family, and he and Pollyanna had planned to take a cottage at the beach not
too far from all their good friends in Hollywood, and
to spend a full month in and out of the water and on
the shining sun-warmed sand.   But the first home-
coming party had scarcely been planned when Jimmy
received a letter with a Mexican postmark which had
changed all their plans.

"Pollyanna," Jimmy had said, "how would you
like to go to Mexico?" and as soon as she had seen

that eager look on his face, she had unhesitatingly answered, "I'd love to, Jimmy. What has happened? What does the letter say?"

"It's from Ramon Moreno," he had said, re-reading it excitedly. "We were in college together. As soon as he graduated he went straight back to Mexico and I have heard from him occasionally since. He has done awfully well. Interested in roads. Well, the dream of his life is pretty nearly realized now. The great highway which is to open Mexico from the United States straight from San Antonio into Mexico City is well under way, and here is the perfectly wonderful part for you and me, Darling. Moreno invites me to come on a tour over the road with him as an unofficial consultant, all expenses paid, and you and the kids might go straight on from here to Mexico City and wait for me there. Why not, Darling? I'll be a couple of months on the road with Moreno because there are some patches of it incomplete, and they offer fascinating engineering problems, and afterward we might stay a couple of weeks in Mexico City jaunting around. And who knows? I might pick up some sort of job down there that would keep us longer. Moreno is a splendid fellow, a fine chap to work with, and I have always heard that Mexico was one of the most charming and hospitable countries in the world."

Plans and developments took place with mush-
room rapidity after that. Two days later, Pollyanna saw Jimmy off on the great American Airlines
condor for Texas. Jimmy's friend Señor Moreno
was to meet him in San Antonio, and from San Antonio Pollyanna received a wire which had resulted in
a feverish packing, of farewells to friends, of buying of tickets and last minute preparations.

"Pack up Nancy and the kids and come along,"
the wire had read. "Moreno has arranged for
ours to be the first family to make the whole trip
over the new road. There will be a government car
for you, and good times all the way. I think you
had better fly. What about Nancy, is she a sport?
There is room for her if she will come. Love to all.
I'll expect you Friday or Saturday. Jimmy."

Pollyanna had had three days of making arrangements and of alternating between Nancy's moods of
outrage, tears, and reproach. Nancy had been a beloved servant to Pollyanna and her children for so
long that she was like one of the family, entitled to
expressions of opinion whether for or against any of
their actions or plans. She had been dead set against
both the airplane journey to meet Jimmy, and the
projected Mexican expedition. Even Pollyanna's
confidence and optimism had not changed her.

"There is nothing at all to be glad about in this,
Miss Pollyanna," she had said over and over again.

"I can't understand Jimmy Pendleton incitin' this family to go up in one of them machines."

Little fat Ruth, in her pink frock, came back slowly into the room, her lower lip protruded, and her round eyes were ready to spill fat tears.

"I guess Nancy is mad at me, Mama," she said, but before Pollyanna could comfort her a big automobile stopped in front of the house. A thin little man jumped out of it and ran up the stairs, and punched the doorbell.

"There's Happy!" shrieked Ruth and Junior in one breath, and they raced out to meet him. He came into the room executing that agitatedly hurried, awkward run that had made him famous in the motion pictures, as the greatest cinema comedian.

"All aboard everybody, all aboard," he cried. "The chariot awaits," and he began gathering up bundles himself, and making Judy and Junior do the same. Happy was one of the dearest friends of their Hollywood days.

While they were loading the luggage into Happy's car, Pollyanna went into the bedroom to find Nancy.

At the sight of the oldish, bent figure sitting disconsolately in a rocking chair by the window, her heart contracted.

"Nancy, dear," she began, but Nancy shook her off.

"I just can't forgive you, Miss Pollyanna," she

said, "taking those babies up in the air.   I guess I'll just say Goodbye to you now, and look for some kind of a job out here.   I guess you don't need me any more."

"I wish you wouldn't feel this way, Nancy," said Pollyanna, "but remember, please, we all love you, and though I don't want to persuade you to do anything against your will, no matter where we are or where you are, we will always want you to come back to us, and any time that you will, I'll send you the money for a ticket to us if it's all the way to China. Goodbye for now," and she stooped and kissed her.

"As a matter of fact," Nancy responded tartly, "I've got plenty of money to buy my own tickets. Goodbye, Miss Pollyanna."

Pollyanna went out and got into the automobile where all the others were waiting. Her eyes were so blurred with tears that she did not see the anxious face which appeared at the living room window just as Happy Bang's automobile sped away.

And, of course, she couldn't see what happened inside the house before they had gone more than a block away.

* * * * * * *

The airport was drenched in late evening sunlight, bustling with activity, loud with the noise of airplanes tuning up their motors.

"Now, Mrs. Pendleton, let me attend to everything. You have your tickets, haven't you?"

"Yes," said Pollyanna, but her heart was heavy at leaving Nancy, forlorn, stubborn, frightened, and alone.

"But she'll come along later on the train, Mama," whispered Judy in Pollyanna's ear, as if she had read her thoughts, "so don't feel badly. Daddy said he was expecting us, so of course we have to go."

"Pollyanna!"

It was Maude Cravath, the actress, middle-aged, beloved, and wonderfully human, who swooped down and crushed them all to her black-satin bosom.

"But where's Nancy?" she demanded. "Happy told me you would all be here."

"Nancy isn't coming," Pollyanna replied. "She doesn't approve of flying—that is, of my flying, especially with the children."

"Fiddlesticks, does she want to live forever?" snorted Maude.

"I feel very badly about it," whispered Pollyanna.

Happy and Junior came striding back, with a smiling red-cap porter.

"Baggage all stowed, everything all set," said Happy. He crouched down, in order to place his round black eyes on a level with Ruth's. All that

year in Hollywood he had been devoted to Ruth and
the Pendleton's. He had tried to persuade Pollyanna
to let Ruth play in a motion-picture with him, but
through Pollyanna's aid he had found a child actor
who had proved so adapted to screen work and to
Happy's own lonely heart, that he had adopted the
child as his son. Still, his original affection for
Ruth endured.

"You're going to get into bed with Mama, right
away," he told her, "and then fly up into the sky.
Like Winken, Blinken, and Nod. While the engine
buzzes and buzzes, you'll be sleeping, and in the
morning you'll wake up, not far away from Daddy.
One more little flight in another airplane, and you'll
be with him. Tomorrow you'll see Daddy."

"I wish you could come," said Ruth, and at that
he held her close, for that was what he had hoped
to hear.

"Telegram, Mrs. Pendleton."

While Pollyanna opened the yellow envelope,
Maude said, "Excuse me a moment. I've a 'phone
call to make. There's still plenty of time. I'll be
back in time to wave Goodbye."

After Pollyanna had read the message, she looked
up with shining eyes. On her face was the look of
joy in the happiness of other people that made so
many of those people love her.

"It's from Jamie," she said, "wishing us a happy journey. Jamie is writing furiously on his new novel in Del Monte, and spends all day on the beach."

Now the crowds in the airport waiting room began to kiss Goodbye, and to wander toward the little covered pathway out onto the broad open field. The great American Airlines plane stood there like a giant moth with outstretched wings. Porters were stowing the baggage into the back of it. Down went a sack of mail, guarded by armed men. A slim, bright-eyed girl, in the dark blue whipcord uniform of a stewardess, ascended the small flight of steps into the plane, and began to busy herself inside. The tall sunburned pilots, in their dark-blue uniforms and white caps, with charts and papers under their arms, were already aboard.

But just as Pollyanna was gathering her brood and marshalling them toward the entrance to the planes, there was a great bustle at the side door of the airport, where the taxis deposited their cargoes of passengers and baggage.

A determined, middle-aged woman burst through the entrance, followed by a taxi-man with a fat suitcase under each arm, and swept toward the ticket office.

Maude was emerging from a telephone booth.

She and Pollyanna called out the same name, in the same voice of delighted surprise.

"Nancy!"

"Oh, Nancy, are you really coming?" Pollyanna's voice was jubilant.

"I was trying to get you on the 'phone and give you thunder," scolded Maude, "leaving these children to go away without you."

Nancy was counting out bills.

"If other people can risk their necks in those contraptions, I guess I can," said Nancy, pale but haughty. "See that you give me a good seat, young man, where I can't see anything. If I see the earth all that way down below me, I'll scream."

"You'll have a bed and go straight to sleep," soothed the ticket agent, "and you're lucky to get this last place. We've been flying full all the way every day. This is a popular line."

"A bed? My stars and stockings."

"I already told you that, Nancy," said Pollyanna gently, "but you wouldn't listen to me."

"I just got to figuring, Miss Pollyanna, that probably if the Lord knew each sparrow that fell he could probably keep His eye on a dozen or so of us humans up there in the air. Anyway, let's get on, before I change my mind again."

Soon they were all settled. The other passengers

entered and settled themselves with papers and magazines. A bride with a bright ring on her finger, and gardenias on her coat, smoothed her new luggage with tender fingers.

Then the door of the plane was shut. Outside they saw Maude and Happy, looking at them with smiling faces.

"Adjust your seat belts for the ascent, please," said the little stewardess, and she sat down in the same seat with Ruth, and fastened herself in with the small round girl.

The great engines roared. Junior's delighted face turned toward Pollyanna's with a smile. Judy was pale, clutching the arms of her chair.

The plane bounced gently down the field, and then wheeled around slowly. The pilots raced each of the great engines in turn—a last test. Then the swift run forward, the uncertain, gentle lift, then the sudden realization that they were rising. Swiftly the land receded, fell away, and the sky came closer.

The passengers unfastened their belts, accommodated themselves to the flight.

Three round surprised happy faces looked into Pollyanna's, and all three said, "We're flying, Mother!"

Pollyanna looked at Nancy. She was sitting with determinedly closed eyes, stiff and stubborn.

"Look, Nancy," said Pollyanna, touching her. "We're flying into the sunset."

Nancy opened one eye.

"Well, so we are," she said grudgingly.   Then, "Looks right pretty from here, don't it?   Prettier than from the ground."

CHAPTER II

THEY were in another plane now. They had waked in their comfortable beds in the big American Airlines condor early that morning, and had breakfasted in the plane on orange juice and coffee. Nancy, though she revealed that she hadn't bothered to undress in her berth, thinking that she would be unable to sleep, had slept like a top, and was a little annoyed that she had nothing to complain of.

Then, after a short stop in Fort Worth, they had changed to another plane, and were shortly afterward gliding along in the sunlit sky near the clouds, skimming over Texas, toward San Antonio.

Poor little Ruth was airsick for a bit after breakfast, but now she had her bright color back, and was peering down at the ground, as they flew, with absorbed interest. Junior consulted with the assistant pilot about air pictures, and tried to take several, though he was warned that he might be wasting his film. Judy sat close to her mother, and was the only

15

one to sense the poignancy of leaving—even if it
was to be only for a short time.

As the plane hummed through the air, she confided this to Pollyanna.

"It's funny, Mother, but I hate to leave anywhere,
and I hate to say Goodbye to anyone. Even for a
little while. Why is that, when I know I'm coming
back?"

Pollyanna drew her closer for a moment. "Poor
darling," she thought, with motherly tenderness,
"she's going to be sensitive to places, and people,
and to things. It's a gift, but a sad one sometimes."

Aloud she said, as she let her kind blue eyes rest
on the horizon, dark with trees down there below
them, "There's a little line out of a poem that expresses what you feel, Judy. It says, 'To part, that
means to die a little.' "

Junior was interested at this, and leaned forward,
beaming for information.

"Happy Bangs told me that everybody began to
die as soon as they were born," he said, importantly.
"You keep dying and renewing yourself all the time.
They say that every seven years you are entirely
different,—all new."

"I don't believe it," said Ruth.

"Well, it's true."

"Prove it," commanded Ruth, and Junior had to retire into a haughty silence.

Nancy was staring down interestedly.

"My, that's an interesting-looking town," she said, and pointed a black-gloved finger. "Look, Pollyanna."

"Why, it's beautiful!" gasped Pollyanna.

They were flying over a little town, laid out in a circle, with wide curving streets. In the exact center of the town there stood a shining white building, flying the American flag, and near by it a pool sparkled blue and green in the sunlight.

Before they asked what it was, the assistant pilot opened the door of the control rooms of the plane, and came down the aisle smiling.

"We'll be in San Antonio in ten minutes," he said. "We're flying over Randolph Field now—the West Point of the Air."

"So that's what it is!" cried Junior, and immediately began focusing his camera for a shot of it.

Pollyanna gathered up her bag and gloves, and put their hats on Ruth and Judy. It was too warm for coats.

Nancy smoothed her black lap carefully with her black-gloved hands.

"Imagine," she said, "Maude has never been up

in an airplane. I'm going to write her a letter about
the trip. Nothing like it to keep your clothes clean.
And no hay fever from the dust down on the
ground."

"Aw Nancy, you weren't even going to come!"

This from Junior, as the plane began to lean on
its side, and circle gently toward the earth.

"Well, live and learn," said Nancy primly, but she
had to try to hide a shamefaced smile.

Before the plane had grounded, Ruth began to
bounce inside the seat-belt.

"I see Daddy! I see Daddy."

As the plane sped along the ground, Pollyanna saw
Jimmy's expectant face. Tall, spare, gray-eyed—
they had been married for a long time now, but
Pollyanna's heart contracted suddenly as she saw
him again, and she thought, "Dear Jimmy. . . ."
There was a man standing there with him, almost
as tall, dark, and slim. He was holding his light
straw hat in his hand, and the sun shone on his black
hair.

"That must be Mr. Moreno," thought Pollyanna.

The plane came to a full stop. Porters rushed
out, as soon as the great propellers had ceased to
spin, carrying little flights of steps, which they moved
up to the doors of the plane. Ruth went out first,
and jumped down into her father's arms.

"Darling baby," murmured Jimmy into her straw-colored hair, for her hat had fallen off, so impetuous was her leap. Mr. Moreno, smilingly and quietly picked it up, and stood by, waiting until all of the Pendleton family should have greeted Jimmy.

"Lo, Dad," said Junior, for he had passed the age in which boys kissed their fathers. They shook hands, grinning, big and little Jimmy, each a duplicate of the other.

Judy clung to her father silently, and lifted up her lips for a kiss.

Then Pollyanna felt her husband's arms around her.

"Pollyanna, this is Ramon. Ramon, my wife, Pollyanna Pendleton. And these are my kids, Junior, Judy, and Ruth. Children, this is Mr. Moreno, a friend of mine who went to college with me."

"I'm delighted to meet you, Mrs. Pendleton. I think you were very brave to bring your children with you and fly in the airplane."

"Where are your children?" asked Ruth, taking Mr. Moreno confidently by the hand, as they started to walk out to a waiting automobile.

"My wife and little girl are in Mexico City, waiting for us," he said. "We'll see them in a few weeks. We're going to go down to see them in an automobile. My little girl's name is Anita. She is just about your age."

"What does she look like?" Ruth had taken Mr. Moreno into her friendship immediately. Together they trudged out across the field, through the airport offices, and to where Mr. Moreno's car was ready for them.

"In you go!" Jimmy bounced Judy up easily, over the doors, and into the back seat. Judy was slight and slim. Junior was to ride in front with Mr. Moreno. Pollyanna, Nancy and Jimmy got in back.

"Your plane was exactly on time!" called Mr. Moreno from in front, as he let out the brake, and started the engine. "We had been waiting for some time, though, because we were afraid you might arrive early, and find no welcoming party. That would not have been in the tradition of my country."

"I can't thank you enough for your plans and arrangements," called Pollyanna. "I feel very honored that we are to be among the first to drive down the road into Mexico, with one of the men who built it! And I have always longed to go to Mexico!"

"We are delighted that you can come," he replied, "and we shall do our best to make you love our country. We want you to be happy with us."

"I know I shall be," said Pollyanna, and Ruth echoed her. "I know we will, Mama."

Behind a dark bower of trees, Pollyanna suddenly saw a cream-colored church tower, and as they passed by in the automobile, a mellow bell began to sound through the still bright day.

"That is one of the old missions," explained Mr. Moreno. "It was built many years ago by the missionary priests of Spain and Mexico. They still celebrate the mass there, on Sundays and saints' days."

"How beautiful it is," said Pollyanna, looking back at the creamy tower against the silken blue sky.

"But you'll see more,—you'll run out of adjectives!—in Mexico," Jimmy warned her, and they laughed out loud for the sheer joy of being together again. And the children laughed too, and so did Mr. Moreno, for there is nothing so infectious as happiness.

So they laughed and chatted until they had come well into the city of San Antonio, and the neat homes, with their patches of green grass and their tall trees, began to slide gently past the windows of the car.

"Here we are in San Antonio," said Mr. Moreno, stopping the car in front of the Plaza Hotel. "There are rooms waiting for you, Mrs. Pendleton. You can rest this afternoon, and this evening, after we have all dined together, we'll reveal our plans."

"Goodbye, Ramon.   Till seven, then," said Jimmy, as he shook hands with his friend.

"Hasta luego, Jim."

Pollyanna's eyes sparkled.

"The first words of Spanish!" she exulted.   "I feel as if I were in Mexico already!"

The smiling hotel clerk had heard her, and as he handed her the pen, so that she might sign the register, he said, "Well, San Antonio is the Gateway to Mexico!   You are welcome here."

CHAPTER III

ACROSS THE BORDER

"We should arrive at Laredo about noon," said Mr. Moreno to Pollyanna as they drove out of San Antonio the next morning after breakfast. "We can eat lunch there, go through the customs, and be in Mexico by one thirty. I don't know how Mexico will look to you at first. I have come over the road so many times myself, that I can't judge it. Yet, I am sure you are going to find it interesting, because I can see that you have a wish to see, and the will to understand. Sometimes, you know, there are people who can look at beauty and see nothing, and then," he said laughing, "there are people like Jim and me who can look at mountains and see roads, or who can see bridges where others see only rivers."

"How long have you been in highway work?" asked Pollyanna, as the grayish green fields of southern Texas, smelling like cinnamon and straw in the hot sun, slipped slowly past the automobile windows.

"Ever since I came back to Mexico," said he. "You know," he said, "there have been three ages

23

of building in Mexico, each one typical of a race, its
aspirations and its gifts.   First, there was the age
of the ancient Indian civilizations, when the temples
and pyramids were built.   Then came the age of the
churches when the Spanish brought with them into
Mexico their civilization and their religion.   And
now there is another age of building in Mexico.   We
are building roads and schools.   I will leave it to
you to assess each age at its true value for if I can
believe Mr. Pendleton, you are poet enough to appreciate them all."

The party was proceeding in two cars that morning.   Mr. Moreno was driving his own car with
Pollyanna in the front seat, and Judy and Nancy sat
in back.   In another car, driven by a chauffeur, were
Ruth and Junior and Jimmy.   As the sun rose higher
toward the center of the sky and the heat grew,
Pollyanna's excitement quickened.

"I have a premonition, Mr. Moreno," she said,
"that wonderful things are going to happen to us
in your country, and that we are going to enjoy it
tremendously!   I don't know when I have felt so
happy to be traveling before!"

Nancy's voice from the back seat was heard putting in the words, "You'd think they would have
an airplane line down here.   Though I don't know
as I would want to miss the ride, anyhow.   Maybe,

I will fly back when we go home. Did you ever fly any place, Mr. Moreno?"

"Why, yes, I've flown quite a bit," he answered. "We flew over the mountains several times while we were working on plans for our road. Once we were forced to make a very interesting emergency landing. We were lost in a rainstorm in the mountains that began to turn to snow. The pilot was afraid our fuel might not last and he brought us down on a lovely little lake. We stayed there a week, living with some friendly Indians in their village near by until two of them could go down out of the mountains and bring back enough gasoline for us to refuel and get away. It was an enchanting week that we had, and I have often longed to go back."

"Are we coming into Laredo, now?" asked Pollyanna as some little simply built ranch houses came into view.

"We are still about twenty minutes away," said Mr. Moreno, and they drove a little further in silence.

Suddenly the little town seemed to rise up out of the bushy desert plain, shimmering in the heat, reflected down from the brilliant sky. Yet the lobby of the hotel in which they stopped for lunch was cool and dark, and Pollyanna's heels clicked sharply against the tiling of the floor.

They had scarcely begun their simple lunch of vegetables and buttermilk, when Mr. Moreno was told by a clerk of the hotel that both the American Consul from Laredo, and the Mexican consul from Nuevo Laredo across the border were waiting for him and his party in the lobby. After the luncheon was finished, Pollyanna was initiated into the thoughtfulness and courtesy which she was to find typical of Mexico and Mexicans everywhere. Mr. Moreno had arranged everything so that his friends had only the most simple and expeditious of ceremonies to go through in order to obtain permission to make an indefinite stay in Mexico.

In the middle of the wide bridge which crosses the Rio Grande and divides the Anglo-Saxon United States of America from the Latin United States of Mexico, a number of Mexican soldiers in the khaki uniforms guarded their cars while the customs officials made a quick search of their baggage for dutiable articles.

It was all over fairly quickly and in a little while, the party rolled out of Nuevo Laredo onto the gently undulating bush-covered plains of Northern Mexico. The road stretched ahead, blue as satin ribbon, and overhead in the sky, great white clouds like blobs of cotton were moving swiftly in a wind that the people down on the earth could not feel.

"We are in Mexico, now, aren't we, Mama?" called Judy from the back seat, but before Pollyanna could answer, Nancy made a tart rejoinder.

"My goodness child, where are your eyes? Don't you see that little burro coming along the road with somebody sitting on his back, and don't you see that little house over there made out of mud with the little Indian boy standing in front of it, don't you remember anything out of that book about Mexico that we read?"

"I only wanted Mama to notice," apologized Judy.

"Out there ahead of us," said Mr. Moreno, "you will see something that is typical of Mexico. Let's wait and see if the little girl will notice it."

As the road curved gently around a few small mounds or hills, a group of little huts made of sun dried bricks and leaves came into view.

"Is it those little houses?" asked Judy.

"They weren't what I meant especially for you to notice," said Mr. Moreno. "Look again."

"I know," cried Judy. "It's that little white house with the cross up there on the hill."

"Yes," said Mr. Moreno. "Every little village in Mexico has its tall church with a cross against the sky so that people can see from a long way off that Christians live there. And even when the village is as poor as this little one, still on the highest point

of land, they have built their tiny chapel and have
set up their cross to give hope and courage to all who
may come there."

"I think that is lovely," said Judy softly, and Mr.
Moreno turned to Pollyanna with a twinkle in his
dark eyes. "The little girl is already sympática,"
he said.

"What does that mean?" asked Pollyanna. "Does
it mean sympathetic?"

"It means that and more, too," he answered. "It
means sympathetic, responsive, and friendly—everything that a good friend is."

Now suddenly they saw against the horizon pale
blue pencilled lines just a little darker than the sky,
and as they rode along those lines took shape, darkened and strengthened, and behind them appeared
other faint lines reaching up still higher into the
pale blue silky sky.

"The mountains in Mexico come toward you
swiftly and seem to grow before your eyes like
weeds," said Mr. Moreno, and Pollyanna caught an
expression in his face that she was to see repeated
many times in Mexico for the Mexicans are devoted
to their mountains, nickname them, and are tender
of them as if they were really friends.

They passed through a small town, and all stopped
to drink a "refresco"—soda pop in a bottle. The

afternoon sun was beginning to decline, and the mountains were darkening to purple all around.

Mr. Moreno suggested that the parties change seats in the automobiles; he was anxious to explain some of the mountain road they were about to take to Mr. Pendleton. So Pollyanna found herself with Judy on one side of her in the back seat, and Ruth's fat warm body curved into her arm on the other.

The road wound about through the foothills and then began a steady climb. The grass here on the slopes was green, and there were bright-colored flowers about, with here and there the curved lovely gray-green maguey bushes. The sky paled to silver and then began to turn softly darker, as a few stars, still bright in the sunlight, began to shine.

As the twilight came on over the mountains, lavender and cool, the road fell into another plain, and then, a little distance away, they saw the lights of a city.

"That must be Monterey," said Pollyanna. "Our first real Mexican city." Ruth's head hung heavy against her arm, for she was sleepy and tired. On Judy's thin little face there were lines of weariness that Pollyanna did not like to see.

"Look, darling," she said to her, softly so as not to disturb Ruth, "there's Monterey. We'll have our dinner and a bath in the hotel, and then a little walk about, and then we'll sleep—our first night in Mexico. Your first night in a foreign country."

"Mama, it doesn't seem foreign to me," said Judy slowly. The child's eyes were dark with some dream of her own.

"So it will always be with my two girls," thought Pollyanna. "One will dream, and the other will sleep. I don't know which I love most."

The town came closer now. Here and there a few houses, and then suddenly a wide paved street, and people walking about their business and affairs. Lovely squares, full of trees and flowers came into view, and then suddenly they were in a narrow street, with low light-colored plaster houses on either side. The houses had long windows reaching to the street, barred with intricate iron work, and within some of them Pollyanna caught glimpses of lights, flowers, chairs and tables. People were moving about in their homes, at peace after the day's work, happy with their own things and their own family around them.

"Isn't it curious how often we forget," Pollyanna said to Judy, "that the world is full of people just like us, busy with their own lives and interests and the people they love, not thinking of us, as we don't of them, and yet here we all are, exactly the

same the world over,—so much the same, that if God
looked into our minds and hearts, there'd be so little
difference that it might even worry him!"

"No, it would make Him glad," said Judy definitely. "He planned it that way. Listen . . ."

Their car had stopped at a signal light, and from
within one of the houses came the sound of a baby
crying.

"Babies cry the same in any language," she said.
"Doesn't that prove that God wants us all the same?
I bet people laugh the same too. And die the
same. . . ."

"Darling, why are you thinking about death?
Has some one been frightening you. . . ."

"No. But I have been thinking about it. Let's
go for a walk, Mama, just by ourselves, and talk."

"We will, dear. Very soon."

The car had stopped in front of a hotel, and Mr.
Moreno's smiling face appeared at the car door.

"Here we are, Mrs. Pendleton. We're in Monterey. This is the Gran Hotel Ancira. You'll be
comfortable here."

Rather stiff and crumpled from her ride, Pollyanna got out. The children were walking stiff-
legged, like little dolls.

But the hotel room was cool. A great fan was
going underneath the light, and the deep windows

were opened onto a balcony, so that the night air
came in, smelling of the fragrance of the mountains
and the flower-filled plazas.   A little donkey was
braying; the sad sound of his voice, dying away on
a dismal tone at the end, made little fat Ruth laugh.
She ran to the window to look out.

"There are lots of automobiles down in the street,
and there's a man on a horse, with a great big hat
on, and there are little boys selling papers, and . . ."

"Come, Ruthie."   Pollyanna got her ready for
her bath.   In the tiled bathroom the water was gush-
ing into the tub—a sound travelers love to hear.
Judy's slim little figure was disappearing into the
bathroom already.

"I must find out what's going on in her mind,"
thought Pollyanna worriedly, remembering her long
silences, her strangely poignant remarks, when she
made any.

The 'phone was ringing.

As Pollyanna took up the receiver, she heard
Jimmy's exultant voice.   He and Junior had a room
on the floor below.

"Pollyanna! How do you like it?"

"Like what, Jimmy?"

"Mexico."

"I love it.   The mountains . . . this beautiful old
city . . ."

"I mean, how would you like to stay a long time?"

"In Monterey?"

"In Mexico."

"Why, but Jimmy . . ."

"Maybe I am going to get a swell job!"

"Oh Jimmy, what . . . where?"

"Meet you downstairs in half an hour. Can you and your little girls get pretty and clean by then?"

"We'll beat you down!"

Judy poked her head out of the bathroom. Her dark curls slung around her damp pale little face. Her eyes were dark, faintly circled in blue.

"Are we going to stay in Mexico, Mama?"

"Maybe. We'll see."

Ruth was winding a towel around herself, before rushing over to the window, in order to look down into the fascinating street again. Some music not far away sounded sweetly; boys were singing.

"I don't care how long we stay," said Ruth.

And as she looked out of the window, along the little streets that climbed up toward the hill, now sparkling with street lamps, and then toward the mountains, purply black and high and protecting against the night sky of Mexico, Pollyanna added, "Neither do I."

CHAPTER IV

A LADY, MYSTERY, AND A MINE

"Who is she?" asked Pollyanna, looking at the tall dark woman who came toward their table. Ruth, Judy, and Junior gleamed from soap well-applied, and had the smooth dampened hair of children lately out of their baths. Pollyanna was wearing a fresh blue dotted swiss dress with short sleeves; Jimmy and Mr. Moreno looked starchy and cool in white linen.

"That, my dear, is your husband's new employer. Are you jealous?"

"Terribly," agreed Pollyanna, as she took in the woman's cool dark beauty. Dark eyes, smooth dark hair, a gentle, pale, but lovely mouth. She wore a dress of white organdy, and round her neck suspended on a small black ribbon, a black cross.

Mr. Moreno rose to his feet as she came near, and held a chair for her.

"Miss Aguamonte, I want you to meet Mrs. Pendleton. Mrs. Pendleton, this is the daughter of one of my mother's friends. My sister and she were in

the convent together. These are the children . . .
Ruth, is it not? Judith, and Junior. And Mr.
Pendleton, my good friend. This is the gentlemen
I recommended to you. You can talk later."

"I am so happy to meet you all," said Miss Aguamonte, and her dark eyes swiftly glanced at every
one, and came to rest tenderly on Ruth's round pink
face and blue staring eyes.

"May I order for you?" she asked, after a moment.
"I know this hotel, and there are some specialties
that you will like."

"Please do," begged Pollyanna.

Miss Aguamonte spoke swiftly to the waiter
in fleet crisp Spanish. Then she turned, smiling, to
Pollyanna, and Pollyanna felt her quiet charm.

"Omelette, milk, and vegetables for the children.
Everything is very fresh, so do not worry. For us a
salad of aguacate, and then steak with tomatoes and
peppers. Ice cream for everyone at the end. If the
children like ice cream."

Three solemn faces emitted "We do," very seriously.

"Bueno."

After the meal had been eaten, and all the group
sat with spoons poised over the heaps of melting
ice cream in their glass dishes, Miss Aguamonte
turned quickly to Jimmy and said, "If Mrs. Pendle-

ton will forgive me, I would like to talk a little business now. After the children have finished their
dessert. If you wouldn't mind. . . ."

"Nancy will put the children to bed," said Pollyanna quietly, for she felt the urgency in the woman's
voice and manner, "and then we can discuss whatever
you like. I thank you for wishing to include me . . .
if you are sure you wish to."

"Indeed I do," said Miss Aguamonte, twirling her
cross on nervous slender fingers. "Because . . . you
may wish to advise your husband not to . . . not
to. . . ."

"I'll say frankly what I think," said Pollyanna
easily, to comfort her, "but of course my husband
must decide for himself. I don't know anything
about engineering."

The fans up above them kept a little breeze blowing gently. Out in the street the pat-pat of a burro's
little hoofs going by, and the cloppety-clop of a
horse's gait sounded against the asphalt. Night had
fallen darkly now, and the myriad stars were gleaming against the black sky which showed through the
window.

The children finished, and excused themselves.
Ruth ran to Pollyanna with her pink lips pursed for a
kiss. "I'll come to tuck you in later," Pollyanna's
eyes promised the two older ones.

"Miss Pollyanna . . ." Nancy's voice was hesitant but pleading. "You'll remember to turn that fan off when you go to bed. . . . It ain't good for folks, sleeping in a draft. . . ."

"I'll remember, Nancy. Goodnight."

Mr. Moreno turned to Jimmy, as the children and Nancy left the room, and put his hand comfortably on his sleeve.

"I took the trouble of recommending you to Miss Aguamonte, old man," he said, "but of course, you're free to refuse the work if anything comes up to make it seem too hazardous, or too slow . . . I knew you wouldn't mind my giving her your name. Besides, you'll see why she needs someone like you at the moment. . . ."

"What sort of a job do you offer, Miss Aguamonte?" asked Jimmy. "Ramon has told me something of it, but I'd like my wife to hear your ideas, and I should like, myself, to get the situation clearly in mind."

Miss Aguamonte cleared her throat, and looked down at her slender white hands. She was clasping them tightly, as if to keep them from trembling.

"My father," she said, "was a wealthy man, and rather prodigal. He was generous with his friends, somewhat credulous. He is dead." She crossed herself slowly, and Pollyanna saw a special brightness as of tears, gleaming for a moment, in her large eyes.

"One of his purchases,—something he bought from a friend, in order to provide that friend with necessary cash in a crisis, was a mine. My father thought it was a gold mine. So did his friend, I am sure. At any rate, gold was found in it. Gold ore. But I am convinced now, that that may have been accidental, and just good luck. There's something else in that mine. . . ."

Here she was silent, looking down at her tense hands for so long that Pollyanna suggested gently.

"You were saying there was something else in the mine? What was it?"

"I don't know," said Miss Aguamonte. "But I want to know. Because it killed my father."

"Oh . . ." Jimmy and Pollyanna both were silent. The sound of other diners, chatting, and eating, seemed grotesque and unreal. Miss Aguamonte was making an effort to control her emotions.

"Father just held the mine, you see . . . for years, without trying to work it. He had bought it to oblige a friend, and he felt that some day that friend might be able to buy it back . . . and he wanted it to have remained untouched, for him. . . ."

"How splendid of him, . . . I mean, your father," breathed Pollyanna.

"Señor Aguamonte was a fine man," said Mr. Moreno soberly.

"Well, the friend died, and we came upon evil times. Many things happened to us . . . Father lost his holdings in land here and there, and he had never saved a great deal in cash. He decided to work the mine. After all, it might still yield a good living for his family. . . . So he went to find it, and to explore it. He never came back."

"But . . . but what. . . ."

"The mine hadn't been worked for some time. The tunnels were old. Maybe the rains had ruined them, . . . we never knew. All we knew was that the Indians who guided my father into the tunnels, and my father, never came back. Something caved in on them . . . it was water as well as earth. There is some sort of underground river that had swollen and had burst through its course into one of the tunnels . . . or something. . . . Anyway, my father drowned, there under the earth, in darkness, alone, away from his friends, his family. We could not even recover his body, though we tried to. The Indians wouldn't even enter the place for two years afterward. They've a sort of superstition about it. . . . The mine is called 'The Mountain of Death.' "

"I am sorry for you," said Pollyanna gently, but Miss Aguamonte seemed not to have heard.

"There is no one left but me and my sister," said Miss Aguamonte, "and my sister is very ill. There is nothing to lose. There can be no more bad luck.

If there is, it can come only to me, for God has already laid his hand on Isabel. I am willing to risk. The Indians say there is evil in the mountain. It is hard to get them to work there. But I want an engineer to drain that mine, make new tunnels, find me what is there. . . . I have borrowed some money, and I can pay . . . I can pay an engineer and some men for something like six months. I . . . had some jewels. It is my will to learn what is there. And I do not think it is only gold."

"Where is the mine?" asked Pollyanna.

"Far to the South," said Miss Aguamonte. "I have never been there. It is about two days journey away from Mexico City, I believe . . . far back in the mountains, where there are no roads, only burro trails."

"Have you any maps of previous work done there, any samples of ore, anything showing the original tunnels?" asked Jimmy.

"No. But I believe that none of those would really be specially useful. You would have to take your chances . . . chances of your life, both inside the mountain from the tunnels and the river . . . or from whatever the Indians think is in there, working evil. . . . I am prepared to pay you for your time, and your engineering work, as I say. If you discover anything

mysterious, and wish not to continue, I will pay you
a month's wages in advance. But I long . . . oh, I
long, to find my father's bones and give them burial.
My mother died wishing that she might some day lie
in the same grave with him. To us, these things
are dear. . . ."

"Of course," said Pollyanna gravely. "And who
knows, there may be security, wealth, waiting for
you inside the mountain. . . ."

"It is called 'The Mountain of Death,'" Miss
Aguamonte reminded her. "Now, I do not wish to
hurry you, but I would greatly appreciate it if you
could let me know your decision soon. Tomorrow,
if possible. Ramon is tied to his road; he cannot
do this for me, now, and I am burning with impa-
tience. I have premonitions. And Ramon has told
me that Mr. Pendleton is the man I need to help me
explore the mine . . . a trained engineer, and . . .
somewhat adventurous. . . ."

"I am no engineer, but I am adventurous too, in
my way," said Pollyanna. "I hope we may be able
to help you. I don't see why we could not at least
make a start. We hadn't planned to stay in Mexico
very long; this is a sort of vacation for Jimmy. But
he is like the postman who takes a long walk on
Sunday. Why could not we say, now, that we will

go to where Miss Aguamonte's mine is, and give her a preliminary report on it, Jimmy Bean? You and I?"

Pollyanna's face was radiant, and Jimmy Pendleton's childhood name, Jimmy Bean, had slipped out before Pollyanna knew it, as it always did in moments of excitement.

"I prefer to sleep on it," said Jimmy gravely, "but I am sure we can help Miss Aguamonte to find someone. If not in Mexico City, then elsewhere. I would like to be of service to you."

"Thank you. Thank you," said Miss Aguamonte with simplicity. "Now I will bid you goodnight, and I wish you happy dreams of your first day in Mexico."

"I will drive you home," said Mr. Moreno, rising immediately. "Goodnight, Mrs. Pendleton. We will meet in the morning."

Pollyanna sat looking at the tablecloth, seeing visions in it . . . Indians marching slowly, slowly up a mountain, weighted down with burdens even burros could not carry . . . the dark opening in the side of a mountain . . . a brassy sun high in the burning sky above . . . then darkness and clouds as the Indians disappeared into the entrance of 'The Mountain of Death.'

"Pollyanna," said Jimmy tenderly, "you're letting

your imagination run wild again. The chance to
help somebody has gone to your head like wine. It
always does. You attract people who need help like
a magnet."

She looked up, flushing, and found his eyes, dancing but tender, upon her.

"But Jimmy, of course I don't believe that there
are evil spirits or anything in the mountain . . . and I
do want to help Miss Aguamonte, you know. I believe that she is counting on this, as if it were her
last hope. And she intimates that her only last rela-
tive, her sister, is dying. Oh, poor thing, consumed
with curiosity and fear, and yet perhaps a rich
woman, maybe miraculously rich, if only. . . ."

"But think how dangerous it may be," teased
Jimmy. "Think of your husband amid those spirits,
inside that mountain. . . ."

Pollyanna paled slowly.

"If it is really desperately dangerous, of course
you won't risk it, Jimmy. We all need you, love you,
too much for that."

"I don't see why we shouldn't look over the situation and give her a preliminary report at least," said
Jimmy seriously. "After all, it will net us a little
more vacation in Mexico. You'd like that, wouldn't
you?"

"Yes," breathed Pollyanna, "so much. Listen."

Out in the street a little boy was singing, and his clear sweet voice rose and fell to the tune of a plaintive Mexican song.

"Let's walk for a few minutes . . . there is a square out there," invited Pollyanna.

"Let's," agreed Jimmy.

The square was quiet now, for it was fairly late. Most of the residents of Monterey were home in their own houses with their families. Around the square winked the lights of shops and hotels, and street lamps. The flowers had closed their petals for the night, but their fragrance hung about the quiet place. A black shadow against the night sky, blotting out the stars, towered above the town.

"Look," said Jimmy. "That's the saddle mountain. Tomorrow in the daylight you will see it better."

Little night sounds were all around. Distant singing, the sound of a little burro sighing and laughing, carriages in the street. . . .

"My first night in Mexico . . . A lovely night," whispered Pollyanna. "I shan't forget it, ever."

CHAPTER V

WITH MEXICAN POSTMARKS

A LETTER from Pollyanna to Jamie and Sadie, and a letter to Happy Bangs.

> Half-way to
> Mexico City.

Dearest Jamie and Sadie:

There's such a lot to tell you! First of all, we're all very well, so don't worry about anything. Ruth is pink and creamy like an apricot, Junior wears me out with his energy, Jimmy is brown and handsome, I'm bursting with good health, and even my little Judy is tanning nicely and getting rosy. My Nancy is the only one who worries me. She is older than she will admit to a soul, though as you know, she scorns cosmetics, young clothes and other such fripperies with determination,—and she tires rather too fast. The excitement of everything we have done and seen, and of being in this strange, ageless, lovely country, has wearied her, but she won't rest. I can't make her lie down, and she insists on waiting on me and on the children, until I'm really distracted

45

trying to make her mind me. I shall make her see
a doctor and get recommendations about how much
she can do as soon as we get to Mexico City. She
hasn't been well for a long time, really.

We met Jimmy in San Antonio, and stayed there
over night. Jimmy's friend Ramon Moreno had arranged a grand surprise for us. That's why we are
here. We are going over the new road—the great
new highway to Mexico City, down which I hope you
will drive to see us. Can't you? Do plan to. The
road is splendid, and though there are not the usual
tourist hotels yet—all tiled baths and luxury,—there
are nice clean little places to stay. And Jamie would
revel in the atmosphere—he'd be sure to write books
and books. I think he would burst into poetry.

He couldn't help it. Such great purple mountains,
wreathed around with steamy white cloud, such a
sky of satiny blue, and everywhere the dark-faced
kindly Indians, riding along on little silvery burros.
Oh, Sadie, the way they look, against the brownish-
tan roads, those little silvery burros with their tiny
black hoofs, and their bobbing ears, with the quiet
Indians, wrapped in bright-colored clothes, sitting on
them, their bare feet swaying with each step. There's
something endearing about them. I can't explain
why. Perhaps it is because they lend to the grandeur
of the scenery a little gently patient and human touch

that makes me realize that I am not just looking at
a beauty unrolled for me as I pass by—I am seeing
the background of living, the background of centuries of living. They draw me into it, make me
feel it all much more richly than I ever should without them.

Mr. Moreno is a dear. He and Jimmy have talked
over college times endlessly. He is a very successful
man, much occupied with his dream of splendid roads
everywhere throughout Mexico. His work has entirely to do with roads. But he is frequently asked
to do other kinds of engineering too, and one of these
commissions he has turned over to Jimmy, if Jimmy
wants it. Jimmy plans to look into it, at any rate. I
rather hope he may decide to take it, for I'd love to
stay here a long time.

Monterey was our first overnight stop in Mexico.
It's a lovely place. The name means "King of the
Mountains," and that's what the city is. Great towering, fantastically high mountains all around, and
crouched at the foot of them, a creamy-pink Colonial-
style city. We began to hear the sounds of Mexico
there—the songs, the people calling to each other in
Spanish, and the sounds of hoofs beating along the
paved streets. It's an up-to-date progressive city,
by the way, with lots to teach us about how to keep
working people happy and feeling that they are really

important to us all for something besides their capacity to work and produce.

We spent a day and a night in Monterey, and then, after breakfast one morning, we piled into two automobiles, with bottles of coffee and some fruit for refreshment along the way, and started out.

Mr. Moreno, who has been busy working on this road for years, and who knows every inch of it, has friends all along the way. It is a tremendous treat to see the country this way, profiting by his knowledge and his position.

I want to tell you about the Indians. They are so sweet, so gentle,—they have such kindly manners, and such natural courtesy. We have seen many of them on the road. They wave, take off their hats, seem friendly and interested. When we stop for lunch at some roadside place, they shake hands with all of us, they inquire for our health, and wish us well. They bless us at parting, for Goodbye.

They are clean, in their white cloth clothes, and what dust clings to them,—to their bare feet, or to the edges of the women's skirts—seems to be just what accumulates during the day, of necessity, while they walk and work. They have wonderful teeth, strong, square white teeth, and their smiles are like light in their dark faces.

Mr. Moreno told us a touching story of the Indians

at Tamazunchale, a village through which the new
road passes. This road, you see, has opened the heart
of the Indian country; many Mexicans, born and
reared here, have never been able to enter it before,
because it necessitated hardships and time, just to get
into it. The coming of the road was like going to
college for those gentle Indians, many of whom had
never seen white men, or understood what excitement and changes the road would bring.

Little by little, Mr. Moreno told us, the girls of the
Indian villages began to take an interest in the supplies of goods that were brought in to secure ordinary comforts for the engineers. And they began to
come down to the road and set up market, and sell
their pottery and weavings and food, in order to get
money enough to buy shoes and ribbons and perfume.

One of the things that the Indian men sell is
cigars—long black cigars, made of the tobacco they
grow themselves. Some of the engineers liked them
very much, and always bought them. One of them
teased his favorite cigar-seller, just for fun.

"Look," he said, showing him an American cigar
all wrapped in cellophane, very properly, "as soon
as the road is open, and all the Americans begin coming here, you can sell lots of cigars. You'll get rich.
But we like our cigars wrapped. Like this."

The old Indian was silent, but attentive. He took

the wrapped cigar and turned it in his hard dark hands and looked at it carefully. He didn't say anything.

But when, after a short trip away, that engineer returned again to Tamazunchale, his Indian friend came toward him with a proud, happy face. His hands were full of elongated bundles of newspaper.

"American cigars," he explained proudly, and offered them.

He had wrapped his black cigars carefully in American newspapers,—plenty of newspapers!—and had tied them up with string.

I am glad to tell you that according to Mr. Moreno, that engineer, touched and a little ashamed of himself, bought all those "American cigars," and made a promise to bring down some rolls of real cellophane, as a present, the next time he came to Tamazunchale.

I could write more—about the little chapels we have seen everywhere, about the Indian villages we have passed, the scenery, the people—I hardly know where to stop, or to begin.

But I must close now. I'll write soon again.

Love to you all, from all of us.

POLLYANNA.

Mexico City.

Dear Happy Bangs:

I am sure that we shall miss you as much as anyone in California. We have talked about you a lot already; Junior is writing to you, and Ruth mentions you constantly.

Have you been here in Mexico, Happy? When we started, you know, we all felt that this was to be just a sort of vacation for us, a short trip, a sight-seeing excursion.

Circumstances have arranged themselves, however, so that I think it is likely that we'll stay for some months. Jimmy has been offered a rather tempting job, involving some reports on a mine, and now that I am here I cannot bear to think of leaving until I have lived here for some time—until I have learned something of the language and the history and the hopes of this beautiful country, and until I have let something of the charm of this city sink into me, and into the children's memories, because I don't want them ever to forget it.

We arrived here, after an inspiring automobile trip down from San Antonio, Texas, over the new road that has just been built connecting the United States with the Mexican capital, and opening up to tourists the most scenically lovely country you can imagine. My husband's friend, Ramon Moreno, who is an engineer with the Highway Department,

and who has had much to do with this road, wanted
my husband to make the trip over it with him,—they
were at college together—and made arrangements
for all of us to come too. Jimmy is tremendously
impressed with the work, and with the country.

And how well we all feel. It is very high, you see,
and cool, and the air is so fresh and invigorating.
We are tanning up swiftly; even your little favorite
roly-poly, Ruth, is brown as a berry. I'll send you
a picture of her soon. How is your Panchito? Don't
let him do too much, Happy. Don't let him be in
too many pictures. With you to tutor him all his
life, his career as an actor is all cut out and waiting—
no need to hurry, is there?

Do you remember my telling you one day, about
the little game that I learned to play as a child—a
game that made a poor little child contented with
what she had to be contented with, and that has
become, with maturer modifications, my guiding
philosophy and my comfort? We called it the Glad
Game. It consisted in being glad of whatever happened, since God loves us all always, and there is
reason to rejoice at every blessing, obvious and dis-
guised, that he bestows.

I had longed to find a doll in the missionary barrel
that my father received, as part of his meagre recom-
pense for the work he did. We were desperately

poor—and I longed for that barrel of surprises,
(though they were only cast-off and useless things
that the churchpeople packed up to send us, hoping
we might find some place or need for them) as a
child does for her Christmas tree. The barrel came,
and there were dresses in it, and other little things—
but no doll. There was only a pair of crutches! I
wept bitterly, but then I remembered the game—I
should be glad. Glad for everything. I was glad
that I didn't need the crutches!

Well, that acceptance, that joyous spirit of optimism and acceptance, I have tried to keep since. I
have even been a little smug about it—I have occasionally instructed people about it, thinking that I
had in some way the key to happiness,—to an enjoyment of life.

But Happy, down here, they invented the best
part of my game! Here is tranquil quiet happiness,
based on acceptance, and that acceptance is based on
trust in God. I have seen it everywhere—felt it
deeply. It has made me very humble.

I must tell you about a charming experience I had,
shortly after we reached here. I had been house-
hunting, in company with Mr. Moreno's wife,—who
is a dear, very warm and friendly and "cute," always laughing and merry,—and we were very tired
when I returned to the hotel. Mr. Moreno, mean-

while, had called and told us that he had just learned
of a place that he thought would suit, which would
be ready for occupancy early the next week.   We
were so relieved, that we decided to have a picnic the
next day.

Happy, what a picnic!   First of all, there was
among the guests, a musician who had taught at the
National Conservatory of Music, and as you will see
later, this proved to be our piece of luck for the day.

We started out in two parties—no children with
us.   As a great treat, they were left in the care of
Mrs. Moreno's nurse (she has one for her little girl)
and they were all going to have a party.   Just Jimmy
and I and Mr. and Mrs. Moreno, and their friend
from the conservatory, Señor Bello, went picnicing.

We started out driving along the blue asphalt
road, straight to the great purple mountains, wound
about with misty scarves of cloud.   In the high shining sky there were many clouds,—thick bunchy ones,
like blobs of ice-cream on a blue plate.

Soon we were ascending a high mountain, and the
clean fresh breath of trees was all around us, and
the scent of fern.   We could see Popocatepetl, changing every moment, and how the Mexicans love that
mountain!   "Mire el Popo" they say, shortening the
name out of sheer affection, and stopping the car to
look.   Ixtacihuatl, too, "the Sleeping Woman," with

outlines under snow as of a sleeping woman under white, is lovely against the Mexican sky. But after we passed over the mountains, and dropped down into a valley on the other side, we saw another mountain that will stand out in my mind as the loveliest of all. Malinze, it is called. You must imagine a green smiling valley, full of little streams, trees, and patches of cultivated ground. The Indians, in their white clothes work in the fields, or walk along the brown roads, and the little silvery burros pick their way along with their tiny black hoofs, their big ears bobbing as they walk.

Out of this peaceful scene, the tall sloping sides of Malinze rise, dark purple up up into the sky, as perfect as pictures I have seen of Fujiyama, but a longer slope.

As we were driving along, slowly, on the road to Tlaxcala, an Indian boy, well-dressed in city clothes, with a brown face like carved copper and heavy ebony hair, hailed Señor Bello.

"Maestro, maestro," he called, and the veneration and respect in his eyes was lovely to see. "I was your pupil, maestro, two years ago!"

"I remember."

Mr. Moreno stopped the car, and teacher and pupil had a warm reunion there on the road. Then, after they had talked, Señor Bello turned to us, and

said, "There is a little fiesta up at Los Reyes, not very
far from here. Wouldn't you like to go—to picnic up
there? It is high—very high. You would have to
walk some of the way, but I think Mrs. Pendleton
might like to see a fiesta—even a little one."

Mr. Moreno was willing, even eager, to change
the plans in order to give me a little taste of real
Mexico.

We went in the car along little cobbled roads, lined
high on each side with that tall columnar cactus that
is called nopal, past little huts made of painted mud
bricks and stones, each its patch of garden, simply
heavy with flowers. The roads got smaller and
smaller and rougher and rougher, as we got into
mountain country where the government has not yet
had time to build modern highways. This was real
"back country." Everything was so quiet and peaceful under the dark blue sky, along those little cobbled
ways, the Indians passing by on their burros, greeting us kindly, the flowering trees by the roadside
scattering down blossoms of all colors and the sweet-
est scents on us, as we went.

Then we came to a little stream. It was dark
brown, flowing along with sandy banks on either
side, and tall trees dripped their leaves into it. The
sun was shining, and it was so lovely, that when we
got stuck in the sand trying to cross it, I would have

been content to just stay there, and watch the little gray burros tripping daintily down the banks, their big ears bobbing, and listening to the water swirling around the wheels, for hours.

But the men got out, and tossed stones into the water, and made a path for me to walk out. Immediately, as from nowhere, many little boys had gathered, chattering and laughing. I don't know what they were saying, but it must have been the same as it would have been anywhere in the world— "Hey, fellers! Come on! Somebody's stuck in the mud!"

But they are helpful, and Mr. Moreno gave quick instructions around, and got out centavos by the handful, to reward the quickest and merriest.

Some got into the water, and scraped up the mud away from the wheels, and some ran to get the great long tough leaves of the maguey, to put under the bogged wheels, so that they would have something firm to run on. At last, after huffing and puffing, we got out of the sand, and Mr. Moreno ran the car up onto a place in the stream where it was hard paved with stone, and there we left it, with other little boys, clutching centavos, standing happily on guard to see that no one disturbed it while we were away.

Then we all started up the trail to Los Reyes.

Happy, you must come some day.   Take pictures
of it! Let people see how lovely it is! Make movies!

The trail, roughly paved with thick round stones
in all colors you can imagine, ascends the mountain,
windingly and steeply, and all along the way there
is the cactus, and the blossoming trees, and from
high up you can hear all the valley sounds—church
bells, and little donkeys laughing and braying, and
children shouting.

Here and there, along the trail, are small chapels—
tiny rooms built of mud-bricks or stone, painted a
heavenly blue inside, open to free air of the mountain and the sun.   Inside them are little crosses,
carved with Aztec images and dates, but they are
prayed to now as symbols of our Christian Jesus,
and as offerings to him daily, you'll find heaps of
fruits and flowers, and touching little designs cut
out of papers and hung up on colored strings.

Up, up the trail we went, and higher and higher.
I was short of breath, and had to rest.   The little
chapels are sweet to rest in.   Praying comes naturally inside them.   You are so close to God, so sur-
rounded with blueness and sunshine, flowers and free
air.

At last, as we neared the top of the mountain, we
became conscious of a steady sound—drumming.
Then, around a bend of stone, and we saw it, high

up on the mountain, far from the eyes of casual passersby in the valley, a great beautiful rose-pink
church,—one that had been built years ago by the
Indians, under the direction of the Catholic Fathers.

It seems to be within swirling clouds itself, so
high against the sky. In front was a bit of garden,
rather run to seed, but sweet still, with old rose
bushes blooming, and trumpet vines winding around
the trees, and with here and there a scrap of molder-
ing headstone, to indicate a grave.

In front of the church there was a sort of rough
arbor, wound with flowers and leaves, and under it,
in front of the great wide-flung door of the church,
an old Indian was standing in front of his drum,
playing rhythms that beat through us all with a thrilling intensity.

"It is the old music," said Señor Bello to us. "The
old music from Aztec days. There is always one old
man who remembers the tunes, and plays them at all
the fiestas. Before he dies he will teach them, by
memory, to some young lad, who will take over the
drum, and the position, and all its honors."

"Bong, bong bong," in fascinating rhythms, the
drum was sounding, high up on the mountain, in
front of the rose-pink church. From inside it came
the high sweet sound of untrained voices, singing
hymns and devotionals.

I looked in. It was a beautiful sight. The church was dark, but the darkness was pierced by the little fires of many candles—all around the high altar, which was heaped with lilies, there were tall white tapers.

In front of the altar, and stretching all the way down the church, the Indian women had made a thick carpet of flowers. Just the blooms. Yellow and red and purple, smelling so sweet, they were laid out, several inches thick, in a design, with green leaves for a border. Around this carpet, facing the altar, each with her tall candle in her hand, knelt the Indian women. They had their heads covered with black rebosas, and from their long full skirts, their small brown, dusty feet peeped out, bare and calloused.

And outside, on the drum that had called the same people to strange festivals centuries before, the old Indian beat the ancient devotionals of rhythm.

Later we went down the hillside again to our car, where it waited in the singing stream, and we drove on to a charming spot where we had our pic-nic, and talked of many things. The history of Mexico, with its roots in ancient civilizations about which there is just now a glimmer of understand-ing—and the next Mexico, progressive, vigorous, and hopeful, with its marvelous programs of education, cooperation in industry, and roads,—its music, its art, and its literature.

Happy, for the sake of your little Pancho, who is Mexican, shouldn't you come here, and soon? Shouldn't you let him begin to blend in with his birthright, his own country, his own traditions? Adopted children do become part of their foster parents, I know, and Pancho couldn't have a better one,—but you should for his own sake, also give him his own country and the background of his blood, besides dear you.

POLLYANNA.

CHAPTER VI

AT HOME IN MEXICO

Mrs. Moreno and Pollyanna knocked on the heavy wooden door of the flat little white one-story colonial house, and waited.

Pollyanna looked around. They were in a small suburb of Mexico City, where all the houses were in the colonial Spanish style—low, thick-walled, with barred windows, close on the street. But inside, where the children would be safe from automobiles, those homes had lovely patios, sun-filled, and bright with flowers, and some of them with fountains, birds in cages, puppies and kittens. A big open room inside the house, a garden inside the home.

Next to this small house, a great cream-colored cathedral towered into the sky. It was marked with the darkish shadows that age leaves on plaster walls. Almost it seemed to have, in the few cracks that marred its surface in front, the old face, with wrinkles of wisdom and years, that God gives those he will soon take back unto Himself.

In front of the cathedral, and to one side, there was a lovely garden, bright with flowers and greenery, and among the plants a black-frocked priest was moving gently, his silvery head bowed in prayer.

The door of the little house opened, and a small woman of middle-age, with graying hair, but bright green eyes, and happy smile wrinkles at the corners of them, invited them in.

Mrs. Moreno quickly explained in Spanish, to save time, that this was the lady who wished to take a house for a few months. Mr. Moreno heard that she, Mrs. Lata, was moving with her family to Coahuila, and wished to rent her house.

It was quickly over. They looked about, and Pollyanna was enchanted. Cool, tiled rooms, easily kept spotless, plenty of bedrooms, a large dining room, a living room, a good kitchen. And the small, but cheery, flower-filled patio. A bargain was struck, and it was decided that Pollyanna and her family might move in, for a month on trial, and longer if they wished to stay. The house would be vacated and ready for them within three days.

Just as Pollyanna and Mrs. Moreno left the little house, and heard the great wooden door swing into latch behind them, there was a sudden stirring of the air, and then a great warm sudden crashing of bells, close and beautiful.

"In the cathedral," said Mrs. Moreno, pointing up.

Pollyanna looked up, but the belfry was so high

that she could not see the great bells moving. Suddenly, as the rich bright sound swirled around, enveloping her in vibrations that struck into the very heart and left her trembling, it came over her that this was a carillon. The bells were playing a tune, singing a song!

Slowly, richly, the melody boomed out, in tones of heavy bells, and all around the sound flowed, like a wind.

She looked at Mrs. Moreno, and was startled to find an anxious expression on her small sweet face.

"What is the matter, Mrs. Moreno?"

"I am thinking of the bells. They will disturb you. The house won't do."

"But I love the bells! I would like to live here, within the sound of them! Really I would."

"Are you sure? They are loud. And if they play at this hour, they will play often. The children. . . ."

"I think it would be good for them to hear that noble music often. . . . Still, I am taking the house only on approval. There would be time, if I found that the bells did disturb some of the family, to move . . . but, somehow. . . ."

Smiling, she looked up toward the tower, where the sound had come from. It had died away now, and yet the silence left behind seemed more alive more beautiful than before.

As they started to walk toward their waiting car, they noticed that the priest had come close to the edge of the garden, and was looking at them with bright kind dark eyes.

"Good morning," he said pleasantly, in English.

"Good morning!" Pollyanna called back happily.

"Are you going to be the new tenants here?" he asked.

"Yes," said Pollyanna. "At least for a time. I am Mrs. James Pendleton, Father, and this is Señora Moreno."

"Bless you," said he, and bowed slightly. "I am Father Mestres. Let me know if I can serve you in any way. Are you Catholic?"

"I am not," said Pollyanna, "but my father was a Christian minister, and we all serve the same God. I will be glad to live near this church, within the sound of the bells."

"We will be happy that you do," he said gravely. He was a tall man, sparely built, scholarly and kind in appearance. His hair was silver white, but his eyes were young in his dark wrinkled face, and when he smiled he looked almost boyish. He had some flowers in his hands, and occasionally he held them near enough to his face so that he might enjoy their fragrance.

He looked up quickly, and with searching eyes.

In Pollyanna's face, not pretty, but radiant with kindness and a sort of eagerness and joyousness that never left her, he saw what he wished to see.

"You have children, have you not?" he asked, and yet he seemed to be making a statement about something he already knew.

"I have three, Father."

"I will be delighted to talk to them sometimes, about Mexico and her history—here in the garden."

"How good you are!" cried Pollyanna. "Thank you so much!"

"Good day," said Father Mestres, and smiled at them both. He moved away slowly among the flowers of the cathedral garden.

"You are already friends," said Mrs. Moreno, admiringly and sweetly. "Everyone likes you."

"Dear Mrs. Moreno! I hope that you will come to see me often in my little house, and bring your little girl."

"Of course."

* * * * * * *

Nancy finished unpacking the last trunk, and stood back, one hand supporting the tired place in her back, and one arrogant finger directing operations as Jimmy bent over the empty trunk, fastening it up, and preparing to carry it away and store it in a corner of one of the extra rooms.

"If I had had sense enough to fly down here all the way in airplane," said Nancy, "I wouldn't be so tired now. I shouldn't get tired just having a few days' automobile ride, and unpacking a trunk or two. I declare, I must be getting old." And she sat down, rather quickly, in a chair, and fanned herself with her apron.

Pollyanna came into the doorway, just in time to see her sit, and hear her last words.

"Nancy! You shouldn't have done that trunk. I asked you to wait, or to have Judy help you."

"The children bother around enough," said Nancy, with the simulated irritation that she always saved for use when she was specially touched by thoughtfulness or love. "I don't want 'em under my feet all the time."

Jimmy had got the trunk heaved up on his shoulder, and was going out with it. He paused in the doorway to call back deridingly, "Nancy should be carrying this out, too. I don't see why a man should do the heavy work. . . ."

"Get along with you," ordered Nancy, and had to laugh a little.

"Nancy darling," said Pollyanna, "when can I make you believe that we want you with us, just

because we want you—not to do anything specially.
You are not to do anything when you're tired. You're
to stay in bed all day when you want to. You're my
substitute mother, and I want to treat you like one.
But you won't let me."

"Why your Aunt Ruth was your substitute mother,
Miss Pollyanna. I'm just your hired girl, and that's
all I ever will be."

"Oh Nancy." Pollyanna's blue eyes filled with
sudden reproachful tears.

"All right, then, you're not my substitute mother.
You're my substitute big sister, and I love you, and
you've got to mind me and take better care of yourself. Have you been feeling well?"

Nancy's eyes fell. Pollyanna noticed that her
face looked a little drawn; her gray hair straggled
a bit; her work-worn hands were trembling slightly
in her lap.

"Nancy."

"Well, I get a funny feeling inside me, sometimes.
Now and again. It can't be anything, though."

Pollyanna put her arms around Nancy, and kissed
her.

"Put your hat on, Nancy," she said quietly.
"We're going to see a doctor."

"No."

Pollyanna got her hat, and her long black coat.

"Come along, dear," she said, dressing Nancy in her coat and hat, and talking to her as if she were a child. And at Nancy's sudden, unaccustomed, child-like docility, Pollyanna's heart contracted, and a little icy finger of fear laid itself along it. Nancy must be quite ill indeed, to give in like this.

They rode quietly to a doctor's office, and came back quietly. And Nancy was very quiet and good while Pollyanna undressed her and tucked her into bed.

Then Pollyanna went outside into the little street. It was getting dark, but she was glad, for she didn't want anyone to see her crying.

CHAPTER VII

JOSE, OF THE BELLS

MRS. MORENO had sent the sister of her little girl's nurse to take over the cooking, translating, and general managing left vacant by Nancy, who was ordered to bed for a long rest by the doctor, to her annoyance and disgust.

"I'll sit up in a chair," she had said, pleadingly. But he was quietly firm. "No, you will go to bed." And to bed she went.

Pollyanna was often in her room. So were Junior and Judy, full of excited talk about Mexico City, and Lolita, the new girl who had come to help. Ruth plodded soberly about on errands that Nancy was too proud to ask Pollyanna or Lolita to do. Ruth brought glasses of fresh water, books, paper and pencil. And Ruth sat long and silently, yet companionably in Nancy's room, on a small chair, listening to Nancy talk about her airplane ride, and the great road down through the heart of Mexico from San Antonio. But more and more Nancy talked about

"when your mama was a little girl," and those were
the stories that Ruth liked best.

Meanwhile, Lolita, vigorous, voluble, and kind,
flew about the kitchen like a cyclone, evolving delicious meals, getting housework done in twinkling
quick time, and taking charge of the Pendleton family and Nancy as completely as it would be possible
to imagine.

Lolita even seemed to know exactly what of
Jimmy's things to pack for his trip to the mine. He
was to start that evening.

When the suitcases were packed, and his traveling
clothes were laid out on the bed for him, while he
splashed and whistled in the bath, Lolita went to
Pollyanna and said that everything was ready for
the gentleman of the house, and she would now go
out to the market to buy some specialties for the dinner before the gentleman started on his journey,
for it should be a very good dinner to speed him on
his way.

Junior and Judy decided to go with her.

In a few moments Judy had put on her hat, and
Junior was ready, and Lolita had wound about her
shoulders a long thin black rebosa, to shade her face
and to hide her arms. On her left arm was a basket,
and to her right hand she insisted, that Judy cling.

Lolita spoke some English, but it was sketchy. However, she had the gift of making herself understood.

As they stepped out of the little house into the long slanting rays of light from the dropping sun, the bells had just stopped chiming some solemn song. Shadows in the cathedral garden were long, and the birds in the flowers were fluttering about restlessly, getting ready for sleep.

"We must hurry," said Lolita, and she crossed the street and started up the block at a brisk walk.

The market was only two blocks away. Around on the other side of the square into which the cathedral faced, there were many little booths and shops, open to the air and to the passing public, hastily arranged and laid out. Behind their wares sat the Indian vendors, calling out their virtues and persuading passersby to purchase.

Lolita walked straight around past the spread-out white cloths on which there were stockings for sale— white, pink and blue stockings, and yellow and black ones—and past the little flat-on-the-ground counters where there were hairpins, knick-knacks and beads. She went to the little box-like, hastily-set-up counters where the Indian vendors sat with live chickens for sale in cages, and where there were fresh sweet-smelling pineapple, and dark green avocados, and cucumbers and tomatoes in red and green heaps.

Lolita bargained in a businesslike way, and ended

by buying some tomatoes. Junior hung on her words and listened and watched; he was trying to learn what the Spanish words meant.

It was Judy, wandering about, slim and little-girl young despite her twelve years, who first saw Jose, and realized that something was wrong.

She was looking at the beads and jewelry, while the Indian woman whose merchandise they were tried to find the English words that would explain her prices to the pale little American miss.

Judy saw the little boy trying to cross the street in front of an automobile, and then dart back again frightened. He was a tall child of thirteen or fourteen, with black curly hair, and dark eyes, a narrow olive face, and delicate features. His clothes were ragged but clean, and he was barefooted.

After the automobile had passed he got across, and reached the sidewalk of the bazaars near Judy. He stood there panting and looking about with scared big eyes. As he caught sight of Judy's interested, sympathetic small face, he broke into quick Spanish, of which Judy caught only the word, "Medico." But, since Nancy had been ordered to bed, she knew that this meant "doctor."

She held out her slim hand peremptorily, took his hot trembling brown hand in hers, and led him quickly, between the market booths to Lolita.

The boy talked with Lolita, agitatedly, and pointed

back toward the belfry of the church. And, though
he tried to prevent them, two tears gathered in his
eyes, and spilled over. "Pobrecito," said Lolita,
softly, and the American children knew that this was
meant to comfort. Lolita patted him on the back,
and then she turned with her market basket to
Junior.

"This boy's father sick. He needs a doctor," she
said, "I go with him. Judy comes. You take the
basket home and tell your mother we will come back
soon."

Lolita's English was melodious as a song, all
the vowels open and singing, and the consonants
soft as honey.

Lolita started walking swiftly down the street with
the silent, sad boy on one side, and Judy on the
other.

"Tell him I'm so sorry for him," begged Judy,
and Lolita, smiling at her in approval, relayed the
message. The boy looked toward Judy gratefully
and said, "Gracias."

Judy's heart felt warm and glowing toward the
boy. "How straight and tall he is," she thought,
"and he walks like a dancer."

Judy loved dancing, and had studied it all the past
year in Hollywood. Her admirations were, most

of them, based on strength, beauty, and grace,—
unusual in so young a child. But Judy was unusual,
—fanciful, impressionable, imaginative, and poetic.
Pollyanna worried about her, because she knew that
gentle, matter-of-fact, practical philosophies come
hard to one of Judy's temperament, and she antici-
pated in advance the heartaches that would come, the
disappointments of the spirit, and ideals that Judy
would have to learn to evaluate only with pain and
tears.

Outside the door of a little light-green house, with
iron-barred windows and a big nail-studded heavy
wooden door, Lolita stopped.

"The doctor lives here," she said, and she lifted
the great iron knocker and gave it a clang. The
sound of it had scarcely died away when the door
swung open inward, and an Indian servant girl, in
a white apron, invited them to enter.

The hall they entered was tiled and cool. As the
darkness was falling, a light burned in a lantern
above the doorway, and in a little niche in the deep
plaster wall a candle glowed in a red glass cup. The
open patio, full of rosebushes and lemon trees, was
cool and shadowy, for the sun had nearly set, and
the patch of blue sky above was already shining with
early stars.

"The doctor is eating his supper," said Lolita to Judy, after telling the boy in Spanish, "but he will come at once."

Almost immediately a middle-aged, kindly, over-worked man appeared, his napkin still in his hand. His eyes were bright and searching, and underneath his close-clipped gray mustache his mouth was very kind.

"Which one of you is sick?"

"My father," said the boy.

"He is at home?"

"Yes, sir. We live in the church. In the belfry. Can you come soon?"

"I'll come at once," said the doctor, after another quick look at the boy.

Judy understood all this. Suddenly the Spanish words had assumed meaning for her, and had sprung into her consciousness as a melody springs complete into the memory.

In a few minutes the doctor was ready, with a small black bag in his hand, and black hat on his head.

The Indian maid held the door open for them, and as they set foot in the street again, Judy saw that it was quite dark now.

She seemed to miss something, but she could not remember what it was. The boy, though, noticed her face, and smiled, and pointed up toward the church belfry, which towered black against the darkening sky.

Then he pointed to himself, somewhat proudly.

Judy did not understand. So he asked Lolita to explain.

"This boy—he plays the bells in the church tower," she explained, as they hurried along. "His father too. It is his father who is so ill."

Judy glowed. He was a musician then!

"What is his name?" she asked Lolita.

Again a hasty conversation, as they hurried.

"Jose."

Judy pointed to herself.

"I am Judy."

"Ju-dee."

They smiled at each other. He said, "I speak a little English," and then blushed.

When they parted near the cathedral garden, and the doctor went with Jose toward the stairs that led up into the belfry, Jose turned and called to Judy, "Hasta luego. . . ."

"What does that mean?" she asked Lolita, and she had to run to keep up now, for Lolita was thinking of her delayed cooking, and the possible anger of the lady of the house.

"It means 'Till pretty soon,' " said Lolita, open-

ing the gate in the wall at the back of their house,
and running across the patio toward her kitchen,
where she saw with some trepidation, the blonde
lady of the house standing over the stove, stirring
something.

"That means, 'I'll see you again,' instead of
'Goodbye,' doesn't it?" begged Judy.

"Yes. That's what it means."

And Lolita started to explain, a little fearfully,
about the delay. But Pollyanna's eyes were kind
and not a bit reproachful.

"I know, Lolita," she said, "and I am glad you
took the little boy to a doctor. I went to ask Father
Mestres if there was anything I could do, and I dare
say there is. That boy and his father live up there in
the belfry. The father is a cripple, and cannot go
down and up the stairs without pain. The boy takes
care of him, and helps play the chimes. He cooks up
there, on a bit of charcoal. Motherless child. And
now his father is very sick. I am cooking something
for the sick man. Our dinner can be delayed. It
doesn't matter."

Pollyanna turned back to her cooking, and therefore she didn't see the look of pride and loyalty that
broke over Lolita's dark face, and was to stay there
always for her "señora", and she also missed the
strange little look of surprised and eager sweetness

on Judy's. For the first hint of that sudden faith and understanding which older folks call love, as it touches a very young heart, is something beautiful to see, fresh and unselfconscious as all lovely things are.

CHAPTER VIII

PLANS, AND THE SPANISH LESSON

FATHER MESTRES called the following week to tell Pollyanna that the sick man in the belfry tower was improving, and that the well-cooked meals she had sent up to him, by Lolita, or by Judy, who begged to take them, were helping in his recovery.

He sat in the little patio with Pollyanna, turning his glass of iced lemonade in his strong brown fingers, and looking with bright kind eyes at Ruth, who stood close to her mother's chair.

"How long will you be staying here, Mrs. Pendleton?"

Father Mestres's English was clear and perfect, his voice deep and charming.

"For at least a month. Possibly more. My husband is now away at a mine, making a preliminary report. He will decide, after this trip, whether to stay on the work or not, if it seems to him that there is work to be done."

Pollyanna leaned forward in her chair. Her eyes were a clear blue, her smooth hair gleamed in the sunshine. She had that look of radiant youthfulness that was always to be hers, even when she was gray and wrinkled.

."But, Father, I believe—somehow I have a feeling, that we'll stay. Perhaps that's just because I want to stay . . ." the lovely face clouded for a moment, sensing the disappointment she would feel if she had to leave. . . . "But I think I've a stronger feeling than that. Intuition, perhaps. Perhaps I am needed here. . . ."

"I am sure there is need anywhere for such a kind lady," said he. Then he set down his glass, and clasped his hands together. Pollyanna was to learn that this gesture of his meant that he was about to say something he felt very deeply.

"I love children about me," he said, "and while there are many here in the parish, I do not see as much of them daily as I would wish, since there are no more church schools. Also, I have not as much opportunity to practice my English as I would wish. I would like very much to teach your children Spanish,—half an hour or so a day, in the garden—if you would like. I would enjoy it very much."

Pollyanna's face brightened as if sunshine poured from it.

"But Father, in your busy days, from among your many duties, to make room for this! I am very much touched. There is nothing I should like better. But, can we not arrange so that you simply send for the children, when you find that you will have a bit of time, instead of making a fixed hour? I don't want them to be a burden, and they are so likely to become one."

"You must not say that," he reproved gently, as he rose to go.

Ruth came solemnly over, and gave him her hand, and walked with him to the door.

"This afternoon, at about half-past three, they might come," he said to Pollyanna in parting. "I teach Jose, and hear his reading sometimes—to hear much Spanish, with explanations, is a good way to begin. I will have Jose come to the lessons. Besides, he should learn more English."

Pollyanna had no more than closed the door behind the priest when she heard Nancy's querulous call from the bedroom.

Pollyanna entered the room where Nancy lay protestingly and angrily in bed, one gray braid trailing down across the pillow, her hands busy with some bit of fancy-work, for idleness was to her a deadly sin.

"What did he want?" asked Nancy, with some asperity.

"He was just calling. And he wants to teach the

children Spanish. I think it was awfully kind of him."

"Well, so do I," said Nancy grudgingly, after a moment.

"Did you speak to him about those dratted bells?"

"Why no. Do you mind them very much, Nancy?"

"Seems like they don't play as often as they used to."

"Oh, so you like them!"

"I think they sound kind of nice. I sort of wait for 'em."

"The man who plays the bells is ill," Pollyanna explained. "His little boy plays them a bit, but the bells take strength, and the little boy doesn't know all the tunes. But wait, listen . . . there they go. . . ."

Both women listened. The young one, with her smooth yellow hair, in her crisp blue house-frock, and the old, tired woman in the bed, in her high-necked white cotton night-dress.

The bells chimed deep and strong, and within the myriad overtones set up by their clangor, the sweet dignity of an old church tune was heard.

It was in the midst of this that the front door knocker sounded, faintly, but decisively.

"Lolita will answer the door," said Pollyanna easily, as she noticed Nancy's worried eyes on her.

But Lolita did not reach the door soon enough, and

in a moment, Pollyanna heard Jimmy's happy impatient voice calling her from the patio.

"It's Jimmy! Back from the mine!" And with a quick kiss for Nancy, she ran out to meet him.

"Hello, darlin'!"

"But Jimmy, you're back soon! I didn't expect you for several days."

"Mrs. Pendleton, I hurried back to tell you the good news. I know you'll think it's good news. We're staying in Mexico for a while."

"Jimmy, I'm glad! I love it here."

"So do I. And I have learned a little Spanish. But right now I'm hungry. Could you get me up a sandwich or something, and some coffee. And I'll tell you all. What a time! Honey, couldn't you come back with me, to the mine? Rough it a bit. You'll be crazy about it. There's a story in it. Wait till I tell you."

Pollyanna called Lolita and asked her to make chicken sandwiches and an avocado salad and coffee, and then she laid out some fresh clothes while Jimmy splashed in the bath.

When he was freshly dressed, shaven, and contentedly munching on his sandwiches in the patio, with Pollyanna and the children around, their wide intent eyes on him, he told about the mine.

"Well," he began, "it takes a day and a half, good

traveling, to get there. A day from here by automobile, part of the time on little-used mountain roads, and then by donkey or afoot on trails that would be marvelously scenic if you didn't have to watch your feet all the time, for fear of slipping.

"It wasn't hard getting Indian guides to lead me to where the mine is. But there they left me. They made it good and clear that they wouldn't go in,—not for all the tea in China.

"It's way back in the mountains—kiss papa, Ruthie! How have you been, baby? A good girl?— in a sort of a tiny valley, which gives you good access into the heart of the hill. The hill itself where the old mine was is as round and perfect as a cone. I suspected it of being volcanic, but I climbed to the top of it, and explored, but I couldn't find any evidence of it.

"I couldn't even get my Indian guides to climb up on the mountain with me, or to set foot on it, though they did stick by me, and keep camp for me in the valley. And they're good camp-men too.

—"Have you learned any Spanish, Junior?"

"No, Dad, but we're going to get some lessons, beginning this afternoon. Father Mestres is going to teach us."

"Father Mestres is here at the cathedral, next door," explained Pollyanna.

"Splendid," said Jimmy. "Study hard, and learn as much as you can."

"Well, as I was saying, the rest of what I did I had to do absolutely without aid. It's just as Miss Aguamonte explained—they are afraid of it. 'Death Mountain,' is their name for it, all right. Monte de la Muerte.

"It's a lovely place. A sweet little high-mountain valley, green and wooded, fed by streams, and this high round purple peak on one side, and a roughish, strangely-shaped mountain on the other side, not two miles away. And the most glorious white clouds, like new cotton, floating across between them.

"It took me a few days to discover that wherever the original entrance to the mine had been, it was now gone beyond finding. I shall have to do some pretty thorough detective work. It will take time.

"But the second night I was camped in the valley, I had got into my sleeping blankets, and was lying down for a snooze by the fire—we keep things cooking up there, over the fire, because it is so high that it takes twice as long to cook anything—when I noticed a light on the other side of the valley, along the edge of the other mountain. So did the Indians. They were pointing and looking. And they seemed perturbed, though they don't show their emotions very much.

"I asked them what it might be, but they didn't know. Well, I went to sleep, and by morning I had forgotten it, but the Indians hadn't. The one who spoke a little English explained to me that he had watched during the night, and that he saw those lights, wavering along the mountainside, all night long.

"After half a day's work around, looking for an entrance to the old shafts—and having practically decided that the stream which gushed out of the side of the mountain around to the north of our camp might conceal an old tunnel, or actually proceed from one—I decided to take time off, to cross the valley, and scout around to see what those lights might have meant.

"It's a nice walk across the valley. You'd love it, Pollyanna. There is thick sweet grass, almost knee-high, flaming with flowers—good heavens, they're all sizes and colors. You'd know more about them than I do. But some of them smell marvelously spicy and good. There is a bit of a lake in the center of the valley, with water the color of jade—something in the water, and the rocks at the bottom of it, and the greenery all around.

"Well, guess what I found?"

He paused to make an effective and dramatic silence, and to give himself time to bite into his second sandwich, and sample his second cup of Lolita's good coffee.

"What, Papa?" Three excited voices asked it. Grouped around Pollyanna's chair were his three, brown Junior, slim pale Judy, and round freckled Ruth.

"Caves."

"Pirate's caves?" asked Ruth. She wasn't allowed to say much, or to join in many of the games, being the youngest, but she gathered up impressions, and remembered things. There was a game Judy played called Pirate's Cave.

"Maybe."

"What was in 'em, Dad?" This from Junior.

"Not a thing."

"But Jimmy," asked Pollyanna, "why all this story then. You must be thinking something about them."

"I do. The funny thing is that they were freshly opened up. Those caves had been made, by hand, by somebody, and not long since. They had all been made within the year, I would say, and from the looks of the ground, I think I know the reason for the lights. Somebody had been digging there that night."

"Curious," said Pollyanna, with a little premonitory chill in her voice.

"How about it, Pollyanna? I'm starting back again Monday. Will you come along? I'd love to have you, and I think you'd enjoy it. The children will be safe here with Nancy and Lolita."

"But Jimmy, Nancy's ill. In bed. The doctor says she needs a good long rest, and that she mustn't do anything. And there's a man—the man who plays the bells in the church. He is ill, too, and his little boy is alone there with him. I ought to look after them a bit."

"Well, when they are all out of danger, would you come?"

"Of course! I'd love it."

"I'll wait a little then. Delay my return. And we can do some sight-seeing together."

"Jimmy, how grand!"

* * * * * * *

The Spanish lesson began well. It was pleasantly cool in the cathedral garden. Passion flowers clambered over an arbor, and underneath was a little bench and rough table. Not far away, among rose-bushes, and plots of daisies, a niche in a living tree held a small statue of the Virgin, and at her feet were fresh offerings of lilies and daisies.

Father Mestres had some pencils and paper ready

there on the table. The birds sang, and the sun moved gently downward in the blue sky, and the shadows lengthened bit by bit.

Judy was dressed in blue, and there was a blue ribbon in her hair.

"Azul," said Father Mestres. "That means blue. Blue like Judy's dress. Blue like heaven."

"Azul."

They all said it, one by one. Ruth's lisp helped her here, for the Spanish people lisp, but Father Mestres, like a good Mexican, sought to correct her, because the lisped Spanish of Castile has a self-conscious elegance to Mexican ears, as exaggeratedly English accents have to American.

Jose was late. He came down the belfry steps hurriedly. He was clean but his clothes were faded, and he looked thin and pale. Judy saw the worry in his dark eyes.

"How do I say, 'How is your father?'" she asked Father Mestres, and he was surprised how quickly she imitated him, and how feelingly she said the words. He was not surprised though at the warm light of friendliness that glowed immediately in Jose's face, for he was an old man and had seen many friendships at the moment of birth.

"He is better," said Jose. By his smile, Judy learned the meaning of those words.

And the Spanish-English lesson continued until the shadow of the cathedral told Father Mestres it was time to move on to other duties.

"Hasta mañana," they all said at parting.

" 'Till tomorrow," said Jose.

CHAPTER IX

THE MOUNTAIN, AND A SCRAP OF PAPER

POLLYANNA and Jimmy stood in the hot sunlight of a bright Mexican day, while Jimmy's two Indian guides, quick and efficient, strapped the luggage that Pollyanna had brought—not much of it, just a clean blouse, and stockings and some toilet things—on a little burro. The little beast looked round at Pollyanna quizzically and flopped his long ears as if to say, "That's not much of a load to carry."

The little town from which they started up the mountainside consisted of only a few little stone and cement houses, with garden fences made of the tall prickly nopal. Everything was quiet, as of the country, and yet not quiet either, for the sound of a little brook running could be heard, and the braying of donkeys far off, the sounds of chickens and roosters, and the buzzing and humming of insects. But of human sounds there were few, because the Indian people are silent about their work, and they are industrious.

"Well, Pollyanna," said Jimmy, "mount your animal. You had better ride now, because you will surely have to walk later."

"Oh Jimmy!" Pollyanna looked ruefully at the tiny burro. "He seems so little, and so disapproving."

"They always disapprove of work," said Jimmy. "You aren't afraid, are you?"

"Oh no," said Pollyanna. She was dressed in hiking breeches and boots, a blouse and jacket, and felt hat, so she felt no terrors about trying to straddle the little donkey. "Here goes," she said, and somehow got herself into place on the little burro's back.

"You're too far forward," said Jimmy. "Move back a bit. It is better to ride them sitting across the back just above the hind legs. Look, here comes an Indian woman. See where she is sitting?"

Down the road came a bit of a donkey, and just above his hind quarters an Indian woman, wrapped in a dark rebosa, sat easily and calmly. Her face was grave and thoughtful, but as she passed them, her smile shone out for a moment. Her arms were full of red flowers.

"I see," said Pollyanna, and settled herself properly.

Jimmy walked. The two Indians walked, easily

and quietly in their big hand-made leather sandals.
And behind Pollyanna's donkey the other little one
followed docilely, carrying the luggage.

Pollyanna soon got used to the ride.   They began to ascend the mountain.   Red flowers grew about
them in abundance, and there was still maguey to be
seen everywhere.   The cicadas sang so loudly that
the ears had to accustom themselves to the loud
humming.

"Look down, Pollyanna!" called Jimmy.   "Beautiful, isn't it?"

"It's lovely," breathed Pollyanna softly, for she
was sensitive to beauty, and the green valley below,
dotted with tiny towns, from each of which towered
a tall church belfry, with here and there the flash of
a stream in the sun, seemed unreal in its quiet charm,
like something one dreams of, and looks down on
from above.

"It doesn't seem as if there could be any legends
having to do with death and destruction and terror
in this beautiful country, does it Jimmy?" she asked
wonderingly.

"I don't know," he answered soberly.   "Sometimes I think that the more peaceful and full of happy
life the country, the more terror there is associated
with death, and the more superstitious the people
are about it.   The Aztec peoples, in the midst of this

lovely country, under this sky and these heavenly clouds, used to fear and venerate death, and make sacrifices to placate their gods—even human sacrifices sometimes.   There is a kind of temperament which thinks that when there is too much beauty and peace and promise around, the gods must be plotting evil.   It's as old as the hills—that feeling.   I've often had it when I was a child. . . ."

"Well, so have I," said Pollyanna soberly.   "I've had it—or a feeling akin to it—increasingly lately. I've thought, 'Here I am, the happiest woman in the world.   I have my husband, my three dear good children, my full life, my friends . . . I have everything, and my sorrows have been infinitesimal.   Yet all lives have their quota of disappointment and sorrow. . . . Mine must be coming.   It must be ahead.'   I even get a little worried sometimes, and wonder if I shouldn't agonize more over small sorrows, instead of always trying to fit them naturally into God's scheme.   Maybe I shouldn't let heaven know how happy I am, because then I tempt God to try me. . . ."

"Sort of like the Book of Job," mused Jimmy. "Well, darling, you know there are some who say you shouldn't make yourself too strong of spirit, because the Lord never sends any one man more sorrows than he can bear."

"Now this is really foolish," said Pollyanna, "be-

cause I do honestly believe that most things happen
for the best. There is always God's reason for everything, deep inside even sorrow. But I *can* see how
a people might get superstitious and fearful, just
because their lives were so good. . . ."

They were higher now. The trail twisted and
made little zig-zags up the side of the mountain.
There was no more nopal, but there were trees, and
patches of ferny meadow near streams and springs.
It was harder to see down into the valley, except
occasionally, between the trees. The mountain air
was cooler and crisper.

"This air is so clean that it seems to me as if it
had never been breathed into human lungs before,"
called Pollyanna to Jimmy. But Jimmy was busy
and didn't hear her—a snake had slipped down from
the tall side of the mountain, and was slithering
across the trail. Jimmy didn't want to kill it unless
it started toward the burros and frightened them, or
Pollyanna. But after a moment, the snake went on
down the mountain, bent on some business of its
own, and there was left across the trail only a little
sliding, irregular track to show that he had been
there.

They ascended higher and higher. Pollyanna,
though still riding, had to breathe hard now, on ac-

count of the altitude, and she put on her jacket, for the wind was cool.

Then, when the trail got very narrow, and rocky and slippery, she dismounted, and went on foot, Jimmy right behind her to catch her if she stumbled, or to support her against him if she got too tired.

"How are you coming, honey? Do you mind it?"

"I'm doing pretty well for an old lady," gasped Pollyanna, but she was very tired, so right there on the trail Jimmy called a halt for a breather.

They looked down into the valley. It seemed miles away now,—dreamlike.

After a time they went on, slowly, slowly. The valley fled from sight as they rounded the mountain-side and began the long descent on the other side.

It was about three in the afternoon when Pollyanna saw ahead of them the little dell by the lakeside where they would make their camp.

The small green lake lapped the pebbly shore gently, the trees swayed and dripped leaves into the water, the long grass was sweet with little blossoms. All around them towered the high purpling peaks, peaks that held secrets, peaks that would hold some of those secrets for many centuries longer.

Pollyanna lay down to rest on a spread blanket. The Indians were busy making fires, and getting

lunch ready. They had had a long fast, and all were
hungry.

"It all seems so fresh and untouched," she murmured to Jimmy. "As if no one had ever looked on
these things before. But of course, they have. Probably thousands of people have come and gone through
this very valley. . . ." And even as she spoke, the
white clouds above her whirled in the blue sky, and
her tired eyes closed. She slept for a little while.
And, being a mother, she dreamed of her children,
and tossed uneasily in her sleep, wondering where
they might be, what doing. . . .

"Lunch, lady?"

She opened her eyes to see Jimmy's thin brown
face close above hers, his gray eyes laughing and
affectionate. He had a steaming cup of chocolate for
her.

"Um, I'm hungry." She sipped the hot sweet
drink gratefully

There was ham, bread, a tomato for each, and
plenty of chocolate.

"Tomorrow we'll have beans," said Jimmy.
"They're already on to boil. Look."

A little fire was established, over which crouched
one of the Indians, tending a pot which he had suspended over the flame by means of a forked stick.

A small tent had been put up a little distance
away.

"Our apartment," said Jimmy, waving toward it.
"The Indians will sleep by the fire.   They like to.
And they keep watch."

"Keep watch?   For what?"

"Who knows?   Don't you remember what I told
you of the lights?"

"Oh yes."

They ate a while in silence.

"Over there," said Jimmy, pointing to a mountain
across the valley, "is the mountain of the mine.   The
Mountain of Death.   I shall have to work over there
tomorrow.   You can come if you like.   But I thought
you might prefer to go over to those caves and see
if you can find out anything.   I wouldn't let you
go alone of course.   You'd take one of the men
with you."

"I would like to," said Pollyanna.

"You mustn't do anything today.   The altitude is
likely to tire you very much.   You must just rest.
But I'm going over to have a look about, before supper.   I'll be back soon,—before sundown, anyway.
Now, mind, no roaming around.   Just lie still and
let yourself get used to the mountain."

"I'll be good," said Pollyanna, with such mock
meekness that he had to laugh.

He was still chuckling as he strode away through
the grass, leaving his footprints behind him in bent
grasses and flowers.

Slowly the day died, the light failed, and the shadows darkened and deepened all around. The quiet Indians were silent about their tasks. The little donkeys, hobbled by having their front feet tied together by a foot or so of rope, were grazing peacefully. A few stars began to shine through the still light-blue sky.

At last Jimmy returned, waving a paper, and eager with excitement.

"Pollyanna! A clue."

Pollyanna sat up quickly, and Jimmy flung himself down beside her, and pushed off his hat. The mountain air had begun to prick freckles through his tan, and his roughened brown hair clung to his damp forehead in wisps. He looked so much like the little Jimmy Bean of her childhood days, before he had been adopted by rich Mr. Pendleton, that Pollyanna leaned over and kissed him.

"Hey," said he, "is this going to be a love story, or an adventure mystery?"

"Oh, a mystery of course," said Pollyanna. "What's that paper that you're so excited about."

"I don't know. But I found it over there near the caves, and it looks as if it had been lately written. See? Ink. And it hasn't been long in the wind and weather, either."

It was a bit of paper, rough at the top, that looked

as if it had been torn from a notebook. On it were some figures . . . dates or calculations. Maybe both. And a few single words in Spanish, set down like notes. It certainly hadn't been written long, for the ink was smudged only in one place, and the paper was still unyellowed from the sun, and hard and firm.

"Too bad we can't read Spanish," said Pollyanna after a time. "I wonder what the figures mean? And who could have written it and left it?"

"Lady, you make the right wonderments," said Jimmy. "Just what I thought."

"Well, I thought we could ask Ramon, or maybe Father Mestres to tell us what they think it means, when we get back. Meanwhile, I don't know why we shouldn't go over there tomorrow, and take a look at things together. It seemed to me that one of the caves had been deepened, since I was here last. I think somebody's digging over there. Darned if I don't think these figures are calculations of depth and distance."

"A treasure hunt!" gasped Pollyanna.

"Well, it isn't a mine, unless this is some lone prospector at work," said Jimmy, "because as far as I can figure out, it's only one man at work over there, whoever he is. But what makes me so nosey about the whole thing is Miss Aguamonte's mine.

Maybe somebody else has heard about it,—is trying
to find it. I am certain that the mine is in the other
mountain. But I may be wrong. Some thief may
be going to get in there first, and file claim. It
wouldn't be hard, you know," he said seriously.
"The entrances to the mine are ruined or hidden or
gone irrevocably. It might be hard to prove prior
ownership if somebody else came along and discovered it, by means of his own hard labor and so on. I
don't know the Mexican laws about it, but they may
have some sort of provision about people losing title
to a mine if they don't work it and keep it safe . . .
or something."

"Well," said Pollyanna. "It looks as if we ought
to watch for those lights in dead earnest, and go
over there as soon as we see them, and ask whoever is
there what he wants and what he is doing."

"He may be armed."

"He wouldn't kill a simple lady in hiking clothes
who came up and said 'Hello. What are you doing
here?'"

"Maybe not."

"Or it may be another lady in hiking clothes, over
there doing the digging."

"I doubt it," laughed Jimmy.

"Anyway, we owe it to Miss Aguamonte to find

out about it, and soon. And we owe it to her to find out where her mine is, poor dear. Don't we?"

"I've got an idea about that," said Jimmy soberly. "It came over me suddenly today. I believe I have the key to that, all right. I'll have to go back down to the village to get some more workmen. I'll need about a dozen good men, and supplies, at first. But I think. . . ."

"What?"

"I think the key lies here in the lake," said Jimmy soberly, and his eyes darkened.

"But Jimmy. . . ."

He didn't answer though, and Pollyanna saw that his concentration on some idea of his own was so strong that he hadn't even heard her, so she did not resent his silence. But she turned and looked into the deep green waters that lapped the shore with renewed interest.

The lake might know. . . .

CHAPTER X

MR. AGUILAR

THE next day dawned clear and cold; the remnants of a light mountain fog were blowing away in the fresh morning wind, and the sun set the heavy dew on the grass sparkling like jewels.

Pollyanna woke suddenly feeling a sense of bright expectancy. She had slept clothed, just rolled up in her blankets, so, after a hasty wash at the lakeside, shivering at the touch of the icy water, and a quick combing and smoothing of her hair with a pocket comb, she was ready for breakfast. The Indian guides, smiling at her speedy eagerness to get her cup of hot coffee and big raisin-filled bun, waited on her with a deference that could not be surpassed in the courts of old Europe.

"Come on, Jimmy! Breakfast! Hot coffee!" Jimmy rolled out of his blankets, blur-eyed and protesting. But soon, over the steaming drink, they were making plans for the day.

"I'm going to walk around the mountain again, exploring carefully, and then I'm going to take some

104

soundings of that lake," he said. "I think that the lake. . . ."

"What about it, Jimmy?"

"Have you noticed that it is fed from below,— there's no inlet. The little streams that flow out from it drain it, but none flow in. Well, maybe it isn't a spring that feeds it. Do you remember what Miss Aguamonte said about the water inside the mountain?"

"Do you mean . . . ?"

"I mean that the only entrance to the mountain and the mine, now, may be from within that lake. . . ."

"But then the whole thing is a failure!"

"It may not be. It would depend only on the cost. Nothing is impossible to engineering, woman. I thought I had taught you that! It's only a matter of how much money can be afforded."

"But if streams from inside the mountain filled up the original tunnels, they should have pressed out through the tunnel openings, I should think. There should be a stream proceeding out from inside the hill somewhere then. . . ."

"I can't find one," said Jimmy. "But there have been earthquakes. The whole thing may have been deflected. Of course, if the whole mountain were hollow. . . ."

"But you said it wasn't a volcano."

"It certainly doesn't seem to be now, but ages ago. . . . Look at the shape of it."

Over their coffee they looked up, and pondered it. Purply-blue, it rose smooth and round and tapering, like a funnel, into the grayish-blue morning sky.

"Miss Aguamonte said nothing at all about a lake at the foot of the mountain. . . . Don't you think she might have mentioned it?"

"We can ask her to go back through her father's papers, and see what mention he may have made of it in letters, or papers."

"Yes, of course."

It was then that one of the Indians had come over to Jimmy, and had said simply, "Look." He turned and pointed up at the mountain. Jimmy strained his eyes against the early sun, but he could see nothing. Neither could Pollyanna, under her shading hand. But the Indian was insistent. He grew excited.

"I'll go get my spy-glass," said Jimmy. "These fellows can see miles further than I."

He rummaged in his packs, and finally brought out a telescope.

He moved it slowly along the mountainside, about half-way up, with the Indian directing his elbow helpfully, as he tried to bring whatever it was that

the Indian wanted him to see into the line of vision.
Then suddenly, he got it.

"By George!"

"Let me see!"

Jimmy gave her the glass instantly.

"It's a man up there on the mountain, digging,"
he said. "Pick and shovel."

Pollyanna gasped happily.

"It must be the man who made the notes," she
said. "We had better go up there and talk to him.
And give him back his notes."

"I don't know," mused Jimmy. "He must surely
know about us. Our camp is easy to see, and there
are more of us. Maybe he doesn't want to talk with
us."

"Well, he may think we're just sight-seers or
something," she said reasonably.

"I believe you're right, Pollyanna," said Jimmy,
after a time. "Let's go up there and be friendly. It
can't do any harm. Still, that's not going to be an
easy climb. And he can get away from us easily if
he wants to."

"He's sure to see us coming, though," replied
Pollyanna, "and if he tries to run away we'll have
reason to suspect him a bit."

So, after more coffee, and after stowing some
chocolate in their pockets, they started across the

fragrant damp grass toward the steepish slopes of the mountain, and began a careful, slow, laborious ascent.

The sun rose higher and it grew warm. Pollyanna's legs, stiffened in unaccustomed muscles by yesterday's trek and the donkey ride, protested, but as the day grew warmer they softened, and she found the going less painful.

The flowers that grew along the ridge they were ascending took her interest,—bright-colored and fragrant, and strange to her.

"Hi," called Jimmy, as they got within hailing distance. The man did not hear them, but they heard the sound of his pick ringing against some stones.

"We'll try again soon," said Jimmy over his shoulder to Pollyanna. "We're still a little too far away, for a man interested in what he is doing, and making considerable racket doing it."

Another fifteen minutes of plodding climbing, and then they came out upon a flat space, at the top of the ridge. It was against another ridge, a steeper one, that they now saw the man, and he turned suddenly as he realized that he was not alone on this mountainside,—alone with the clouds and the flowers and the sound of his pick, and his own secret thoughts.

"Hi," called Jimmy. "Hello there!"

The man, bare-headed, dark and slim, rested on

his pick, and answered gaily enough, "Hello to you! What are you doing up here?"

"We came up here to find you," said Pollyanna simply. "We saw you from our camp down below, and we wondered what you were doing."

"I'm . . . I'm digging," he said, flatly, and then he laughed, as if he knew that was no answer.

He was dark-eyed, bronze-skinned. He wore horn-rimmed spectacles, and his face was that of a student, gentle and dreamy, but his mouth seemed used to smiles and his eyes knew humor.

"I'm a lawyer, Juan Aguilar," he said. "I come up here on vacations. My home is Mexico City. You're Americans, aren't you? I went to college in the states, for two years. But I came home to finish."

"I'm James Pendleton," said Jimmy. "This is my wife. I'm an engineer. Doing a bit of work here. That is, I may. I'm just looking over some possibilities."

The man's face clouded with some quick distressing thought.

"Yes? What kind of work . . . what kind of possibilities?" he asked, politely, but with an undercurrent of worry in his voice.

Jimmy heard that worry, but he preferred not to interpret it correctly.

"I'm not at liberty to say," he answered easily,

"but I can tell you this, which as a Mexican I suppose you'd like to know. I am working for a Mexican concern, and any exploitation my work may lead to, will be Mexican, and for Mexico. I quite sympathize with you that your own resources should remain within the country, to benefit yourselves."

The man smiled quickly and delightedly.

"But of course," he said gracefully. Then suddenly, he turned, and looked at them both very frankly.

"I may as well tell you what I am doing," he said, after a moment, "since I have a permit to do it, and you may be interested in helping me. Have you been long in Mexico? Do you like the country?"

"We haven't been here long," said honest Pollyanna, "but we love your country. We want to stay as long as we can."

"Well, I am a sort of amateur archæologist," said Mr. Aguilar. "I think I am on the track of something rather marvelous—here in these mountains. But I have little to go on besides some researches into history and legend that I have made. Those researches lead me here, but I am like the man in your saying who searched for needles in haystacks? How to look? I have no clues."

"I don't suppose you have much time either," said

Jimmy, "if you have a practice in Mexico City. It takes time even getting here."

"That's true," said Mr. Aguilar, sitting down with a sigh, and taking out cigarettes, which he passed to Jimmy. Pollyanna, seated on the grass, listened like a quiet child, and made little chains of the flowers she could pick from the sward without even rising, but they quickly faded from the warmth of her hands as she worked with them, and she soon stopped, and just let her hands rest idly in her lap. It was glorious looking down across the valley, anyway, and the things that the men were saying,— interesting enough,—flowed through her consciousness without leaving an imprint. She was thinking of the children, Nancy, the patio. . . . Already the little house by the cathedral was home, and she felt a stirring of nostalgia for it.

"I've had a hunch that there were magnificent keys to an old civilization here," said Mr. Aguilar, puffing nervously at his cigarette. "The legends of the place . . . you know the legend of 'The Mountain of Death'?"

"We've heard of it," said Jimmy. "The Indians fear the place. I'll have the dickens of a time getting laborers, if I find what I'm looking for here, and try to get under way working."

Mr. Aguilar turned to him frankly.

"Let's be completely frank with each other," he begged suddenly. "I don't think we're after the same thing at all, and each of us may be able to help the other. You'll have to take me on trust, but I've a few letters here, some cards. . . ." He began to fumble in his jacket.

But Jimmy stopped him with a gesture and a laugh.

"Look here. You and I are both used to judging men. You as a lawyer, I as an engineer. I trust you not to say anything about my work here, and I'll be careful of your confidence. And we might overlap a bit. We might be of great help to each other. And you're doing me rather an honor to suggest this confidence first, for of course you are in your own country and have every right here. I am simply a foreigner, employed for a certain commission. If you will take my wife into our conference. . . ."

Mr. Aguilar looked for only one moment into Pollyanna's guileless eyes, and then he answered immediately, "Of course."

"Well then," said Jimmy, "I am looking for a lost gold mine that I believe to be hidden in this very mountain. My employer is a Miss Aguamonte of Monterey. Her father, so she told me, took over a mine for a friend who needed ready cash, and then, out of friendship, did not work it, thinking that his friend would wish to reclaim it when he could get his fortunes together again. But the friend died, and Miss Aguamonte's father fell on hard times. He came to look over his property. But something happened—nobody knows just what—Miss Aguamonte thinks that some sort of inner spring in the mountain gathered force, burst through the tunnels of the mine and drowned her father. Or the tunnels caved. But the Indians through whom she eventually got the sad news of her father murmured something to do with water.

"She is poor now, but she borrowed something, and she wants me to find that mine, and open it up, work it if possible. And she wants to find her father's bones, and give them burial."

Mr. Aguilar was silent a long time.

"This is very strange," he said at last, in a curious voice, and he looked at them with curious, startled eyes. "This is very strange."

CHAPTER XI

THE GARDEN, AND THE BELFRY

It was nearly three o'clock, and Father Mestres had told the children to come for a lesson that afternoon. Judy stood in her mother's bedroom, before the mirror and tied her hair-ribbon. She had put on a fresh blue dress,—dotted swiss and made with ruffles—and the ribbon matched the dress and her eyes. She worriedly twisted her dark hair into ringlets, and wound the ribbon between them. Then she stealthily opened Pollyanna's powder box, and took out the puff, and stood there, half fearful with it poised above her small nose.

"What goes on?" asked Junior disapprovingly from the doorway.

Judy flushed. She had just about decided not to put on even a flick of powder, for she knew that Pollyanna wouldn't approve of it for a twelve-year-old, but now at the coarse male bossiness in Junior's voice, she knew that she must put it on, be the punishment what it might. She calmly fluffed on the powder, and smoothed it across her cheeks.

"Fooey," said Junior. "Flour barrel."

Ruth had come in from the patio; she was always anxious to catch up. Always eager to be where the excitement was, and part of the fun.

"Look," said Junior, taking Ruth in on his side. "Judy's putting Mama's powder on."

Ruth rushed over and held up her round sunburnt face. "I want some," she said.

"Hey," said Junior. "Father Mestres won't like that."

"No," said Judy suddenly. "He wouldn't."

She had a feminine wile of unbending gracefully and completely when she must. "All right then Junior. I'll take it off. I wasn't going to put it on anyway. I was just thinking. But you made me mad. I'm sorry though." And she flashed her smile at him, a smile that was already beginning to take on the comradely and yet evanescent sweetness that was to be one of her devastating charms when she grew into young womanhood.

"Well," said Junior, "you'd better mind me when Mama and Dad are away, anyhow. I'm the oldest and the man of the house."

Judy preferred to let this boasting pass.

She finished tying her ribbon.

"Junior," she wheedled, in a soft voice, looking up at him from under her lashes, "do you think

Mama would mind if I put on one tiny drop—just one—of her perfume?"

"Well. . . ." He hesitated. Then, "Lemme smell it," he demanded.

Judy held out the bottle.

"I think it's a little too sophisticated for you," he pronounced.

"Only a tiny drop. . . ."

"Well . . . one then."

Judy put one on, carefully.

Ruth held out the ruffle round the neck of her fat yellow frock. "I want a drop of Mama's perfume, too."

Judy's wiles were instinctive.

"Can I give her one, Junior?" she appealed to the self-constituted authority.

He was pleased to be magnanimous. "Aw, give her one," he ordered, with careless good humor, and Judy dropped one globule of sweetness on Ruth. Ruth buried her nose in her dress, and sniffed ecstatically.

"I'm going to let Nancy smell me," she said, and ran as hard as she could, her small feet pattering wildly along the tiles, to where Nancy lay in bed, impatiently knitting.

"I'm going to take my camera over today," said Junior, "and try to make some pictures of Father

Mestres and the Church. The shadows and sunlight in the garden should be hard to get."

"But you're so good getting hard effects," said Judy. "Why don't you ask Jose to let you go up in the belfry with him? I bet you could take some lovely scenes from up there."

The bells were singing now, to chime the mid-afternoon. The sweet loud clangor filled the room like a tide.

As soon as it was silent, Nancy called.

"I'm coming," caroled Judy, and skipped into the room where Nancy lay, her bed close to the window.

"Let me see how you look."

Judy revolved slowly.

"You look very nice," said Nancy. "Kinda interested in prettifyin' yourself lately, aren't you?"

Judy darkened to her hair.

"'Bout time," said Nancy.

Nancy looked pale and tired. Her hair was done up in a knot on top of her head, and she was half-sitting up, wearing a bed jacket of pink wool but she still looked ill. In her busy fingers was a bit of wool and some needles.

Judy, child though she was, noticed that Nancy looked haggard.

"Would you rather I stayed home and read to you, or something, Nancy?" she offered.

"No darling. You better go learn your lesson."

"Come on, if you're coming," called Junior from the doorway. "It's time to go, and Father Mestres is out there in the garden waiting."

He looked at Judy speculatively as they opened the big front door and stepped out into the golden sunshine.

"I wish I knew who you were dressing up for," he mused, with sudden brotherly suspicion.

"Walk faster Ruthie," said Judy to the fat little sister, "and stop smelling your dress."

Father Mestres smiled at the three. He was ready with paper and four pencils.

"We'll have a list of words today," he said. "I hope you remember all the words I taught you. Ruth need not write. She can just think and remember. We will have a private lesson when the others are through. Ruth, you may go now and pick some flowers for me. I want fresh flowers for the altar of St. Joseph."

"But Jose is not yet here," murmured Judy, as she sat down and arranged her blue skirts.

"He is coming," said Father Mestres, and sure enough, there he came, walking quickly along the path between the high flowers. He was hatless, and

his white blouse was unbuttoned at the neck. His
mended and patched trousers were freshly brushed,
and he wore shoes, though he had no stockings.

But Judy saw only the sun on his hair, and his
brown eyes, and a sort of aura around him.

"Father Mestres," she said, "Jose really looks
like a musician, doesn't he?"

He looked down into the ecstatic small face, into
those adoring eyes that shone on the boy, and he
smiled with a sort of pitying tenderness.

"Jose is nice-looking," he said, "and he is a good
boy. A very good boy."

"Buenos dias, Padre," said Jose, and then to the
children the English greeting. "Good afternoon."

The lesson proceeded, while the bees hummed
lazily among the flowers, and an occasional cloud,
sailing by overhead, cast a momentary shadow over
the little group at the rough board table in the cathedral garden.

"Here is a bunch I picked," said Ruth, and she
came toward Father Mestres with her fat fist
clenched so tightly round the blossoms that the
perspiration burst out between her small fingers.

"St. Joseph will be pleased," said Father Mestres.
"Thank you."

"I'll go now and pick some more," said Ruth.
"I'll go home, and pick some in our own patio."

And she started away.   But they had not heard her
last words, and nobody told her she must not cross
the street alone.   Jose was writing down English
words, and Judy and Junior were working out a sen-
tence in Spanish.

When at last Father Mestres gathered up his
pencils and said, "I think that will be all for today.
We can have a little time again the day after tomorrow," they had forgotten Ruth.

Junior, in halting Spanish, asked Jose if he might
come with him, up into the belfry.   Judy longed to
go, but she was too proud to ask.   She stood there,
hopeful, silent, praying.

Jose turned to her, and said, "Tu tambien."   You
too.

Judy's heart burned with pleasure.

"I would love to see the bells," she murmured.

"I will show you," said Jose.   "I will also play
for you, if you can stay until the time for evening
song.   Only an hour.   My father will wish to speak
with you and send thanks to your kind mother.   He
is better now.   He will soon play the bells again."

Junior drew out his camera, and ran after Father
Mestres just before the priest reached a small side
door and was about to enter the church.   They spoke
a moment together, and then Father Mestres stood
where he was, quietly smiling, his black gown etched

strongly against the creamy wall of the church, the blossoming roses waist-high around him, while the boy sighted and arranged his camera.

Then Junior came back, and the three children began to ascend the belfry steps. They were high stone steps, and twisting. It seemed dark inside the church after the brilliant sunshine of the afternoon—cool, too. But a tiny shaft of light from a narrow window hung down dancing with motes, across the darkness, as palpable as a piece of yellow satin.

"Where's Ruth?" asked Junior. "Is she coming?"

"These steps are too high for her," said Judy. "She's in the garden picking flowers. She'll be all right. We can call to her from the top of the church."

"You know she'll want to come up."

"Well if she does, she can," said Judy easily.

They came out onto a sort of lookout. The cathedral had been built in conjunction with a convent, but some of the convent had fallen into disuse, and part of it had been ruined in a quake. Only a few rooms of it were still standing, and the great wide balcony, open to the air, that was called a "mirador." It was here that Jose and his father had their simple establishment.

On the mirador, back toward the wall, they had a tiny charcoal burner, and a few dishes and supplies.

"That's where we cook," said Jose, waving a
brown hand toward it.

"In there, there are cells, where the monks used
to live. We have our bedrooms there."

Judy went to the railing of the mirador and
looked out. It was high. She could look over the
rooftops of the little suburb, down on the plaza,
where people and horses were passing by, over the
gardens. She could see the spires and housestops of
Mexico City, there in the distance, and the rim of
dark mountains on the other side of the valley.

"How lovely to live up here, high, high up, by the
clouds and the sun," she said.

"Sometimes I think I don't belong with people
down on the ground," said Jose. "But I have to go
to school in the winter. Then I feel more like them.
In the summer, I hardly ever think of people."

"How is your father today?"

"He is better. He is resting in his room."

Junior was delighted. He was sighting his camera from various angles. He was running from one
spot of vantage to another, calculating lights and
distances.

"Jose, will you show me the bells?"

"Certainly."

He led the little girl into the small belfry room.
There they were, all the great bells, copper-colored

some, others gray like lead, and some were greenish. From them hung down leather thongs, attached to the clappers, and these were rigged up on a simple machine, so that the bells could be sounded by pulling levers on the floor.

"Soon," said Jose, looking out at the sky, and noticing that the sun was falling down across the sky toward the earth now, "soon it will be time for evening song, and if you like you can watch me play. I can't play like Father, but I know some songs."

"I wish I could learn to play," said Judy.

He laid a finger on her slim arm.

"You wouldn't be strong enough," he said, shaking his head. "I am thin, but I am strong. Look, it takes strength to pull these. There are some that I cannot pull. You have to move that weight up there, you see,—that clapper. On the big bells, that weighs many pounds."

"It's wonderful to be able to make music with those bells," she gasped.

They talked, and Junior took pictures, until time for the evensong. They spoke to Jose's father, but he could only smile and wave at them, for he knew no English.

"They have bells like these, only more in many great churches," said Jose to Judy, "my father tells

me.   In your country there are some fine bells, and
in France, and Spain.   When I am older I wish to
travel and see all those bells.   I wish to play on them,
and learn to be one of the best.   I want to be a great
bell-player, that people will come miles to hear. . . ."

"Oh, I know you will," said Judy softly.   "I know
you will."

And she stayed while he played the evening song.
It was loud, terrifying, there in the growing dark,
with the wild sound all around her.   But she was
near Jose.   She felt that she would never forget that
half-hour in the bell tower.   And she never did.

CHAPTER XII

A LOST CHILD

It was suddenly quite dark when Judy decided that she must go home.

"We'll come soon again," she and Junior promised as they began to feel their way down the dark steps inside the tower that led into the belfry.

"Tomorrow," begged Jose.

"Yes. We'll come tomorrow."

"Hasta mañana, Jose."

"Hasta mañana, amigos."

Clouds had gathered, to dull the sunset, and rain threatened. The air was dampish and expectant. Before they had left the cathedral gardens, big drops began to spatter down, knocking dust off the leaves of the plants, splashing on the stones.

Suddenly Judy stood stock still, and her heart fell. She clutched Junior.

"Where's Ruthie?" she whispered.

"You said she was picking flowers."

"I forgot her. She can't be here. We would have heard her."

125

Junior rushed out in front of the church, and looked. "Ruth! Ruth!"

Judy began calling too. The rain was coming fast. The trees began to shake in a wind.

"Maybe she's home. We'd better run home and see."

They opened the door of their house, and burst through the hall into the patio. There was already a light burning in the hall, and lights from the kitchen and dining room, and from Nancy's room streamed out into the patio. But there was no answer to their calls, except Lolita, who came rushing out of the kitchen, aproned and spoon in hand.

"Is Ruth here?" quavered Judy.

"She was with you," answered Lolita worriedly. "Why? Is she lost?"

"Oh . . ." Judy began to tremble and cry. "What'll we do, Junior?"

"I'm going to get my coat on and go out looking for her," he answered shortly, and ran into his room to get one.

Judy's sobs rose.

"I'm going with you. I forgot my little sister. Oh, Mother will never forgive me. How could it happen when I was so happy. . . ."

"If you're coming with me, you'd better put on

something warm." He held out Judy's coat, and
helped her into it. In his seriousness and quietness
now he resembled his father.

"What's all this?"

Nancy stood in the doorway of her room, in her
nightgown, her feet on the cold tiles, with a shawl
held over her shoulders.

"We're going out to look for Ruth."

"Isn't she with you?"

"She was in the garden with us . . . and then we
went upstairs with Jose, and left her in the gardens
. . . and . . . when we came down again . . . she was
gone."

"That was hours ago!" Nancy's voice rose on a
high-pitched, nervous note.

"I know." Judy's tears flowed.

"I'm going." Junior flung on ahead, and they
heard the front door slam to after him.

"You stay here, Miss." Nancy was severe. "We
don't want to have to look for two. Go into your
room, and stay there."

"Nancy, you're sick. Mama wouldn't want you
to be up. Oh, Nancy, please, you mustn't."

"Don't tell me what to do, Miss, you that can't
even watch your little sister, and lets her go off wandering in the dark."

"Please Nancy, your going out won't help."

"She will always come to me when I call her. I'm going out. Here, help me fasten my skirt."

Despite Judy's protests, Nancy was struggling into her stockings, her shoes. Holding herself upright, for she was swaying and weak, she got into her petticoat, her woolen skirt. She had lost weight lying in bed; the skirt hung down from her waist, and was loose. The little girl, though her eyes were blurred with tears, could hook it easily.

Nancy buttoned up a blouse, and pulled on a jacket. She clapped on a hat. She took her purse out of the top bureau drawer.

"Nancy, it's raining. Please don't go out."

"My precious lamb, out in the rain, lost. . . ." Nancy was hurrying through the hall.

Lolita was at the door ahead of them, her rebosa around her head.

"I will go to the police," she said. "I can explain quickly in Spanish. They will quickly find the baby."

Nancy locked the door behind them, and she and Judy started out.

"First we'll look again in the church gardens," said Nancy. "She might have fallen asleep somewhere."

While Nancy beat about in the dark bushes, clutching her coat together, and calling through the falling rain, Judy went into the church, dark and quiet, and smelling faintly sweet from all the incense that had been burned in it for years on end.

"Ruth," she called timidly, and her own voice came echoing back to her out of the dark.

"Ruth!"

There was no answer.

She came out to find Nancy impatiently looking for her.

"She can't be here," worried Nancy. "I've looked everywhere. We'll look in the plaza next. There are benches and things over there. I can't help thinking she must have fallen asleep somewhere. She can't talk Spanish. . . ."

"You don't think . . . anybody could have taken her?" Judy was shaking; her eyes were dry now, but little sobs shook in her throat.

"Of course not. Whatever for, a fat baby like that?"

But the plaza, deserted because of the rain, save for a few Indians who sat under a thick tree that kept them safe from the pelting drops, was empty. There was no little girl. They even looked, trembling with dread, into the pool below the fountain, but it was dark green, and tranquil save for the raindrops falling into it.

"Well, we'll just have to go up and down asking

for her at every house," said Nancy. "How do you say, 'Have you seen a little girl?' Quick now, you've learned that much in those lessons, I hope."

" 'Ha tristo una niña?' I think you would say," answered Judy. "I am sure anyone would understand."

They knocked at the door of the house next to theirs, but there was no answer.

At the house next that, the man who came to the door was sympathetic and kind, but his shrug said as well as words that he hadn't seen any little girl.

All down the block it was the same story. All back the block, on the other side of the street, it was the same. A few passersby, who looked curious, shrugged, looked blank, or blankly sad.

Here came Lolita, with a policeman.

"The police are looking now," she said. "You must go home, both. The police can do more than we."

"I can't go home," said Nancy, and her voice broke.

"You must come," said Lolita kindly but firmly, and turned her about, and led her quickly back to the little pink house near the cathedral.

They went into the hall, and Lolita guided Nancy straight to her room, and began methodically undressing her.

"You must go in bed," she said severely. "You should not get up."

And before Nancy knew it, the kind brown fingers had got her into her nightgown, and had tucked her up warmly in bed, and soon a cup of steaming hot chocolate was ready for her.

"I can't think of eating until I hear some good news," said Nancy, but Lolita was patient.

"Drink," she said, and Nancy drank a bit. The hot sweet liquid warmed her, gave back a little hope. She relaxed into the warm bed.

Lolita turned to Judy then.

"You will have a hot bath," she said. "The water prepares itself. Then the chocolate, too. In bed."

"Lolita, you are so good to me, and I'm so bad."

Judy's crying burst out, tragic with the tragedy of youth, when it feels guilty and helpless.

"Probecita." Lolita comforted her sweetly. "The Good Lord will forgive."

It was when Judy was in bed, taking her chocolate, though she still sobbed and hiccuped, and the hot drink did not help this, that Junior burst in, with two policemen, and Ruth, and a distracted and upset little man in a white apron.

"Hey! Everybody! The lost is found!"

Nancy and Judy rushed out, in dressing gowns. Lolita sped in from the kitchen.

"I've got cakes," said Ruth, proferring a large paper bundle she was carrying. "I made 'em."

"But baby darling, where have you been?" Nancy was holding her so tight, that Ruth could scarcely answer.

"I was with him," said Ruth, fat and happy, pointing to the little man in the apron, who smiled sheepishly. Her pink cheeks were warm and sugary, and there was sugar around her lips.

"He bakes cakes. I went to see him today, and he let me bake some."

The little man spoke quickly with Lolita.

Lolita dismissed the policemen, with many thanks and bows, and then explained, and translated.

The little baker was very sorry to have worried her parents. He was thoughtless. The little girl came in, through the back door of the shop, and stood watching him, in the afternoon. She couldn't speak Spanish, but she could make herself understood. He gave her some cookies. He let her make some cookies. She stayed while they were baking. She was so sweet, he forgot about the time, and her mother and father worrying. He was most unhappy to have caused worry. But his wife and he—they loved children. And she spoke no Spanish. They couldn't ask her where she lived. . . .

"Never mind. Never mind. Everything's all right now."

Nancy thanked him, and so did Judy. They walked with him to the door, and thanked him again. They looked on him as a saviour.

And then, nurselike and motherlike, Nancy released her worry.

"You're a bad girl," she said to Ruth fiercely, "to stay away so long! Why didn't you come home?"

Ruth's little face wrinkled up like a crinkled rose-leaf into impending tears.

"I was making you a cake. . . ."

"All right, baby. Never mind. We'll eat the cakes tomorrow."

* * * * * * *

Judy got out of bed later that night, and knelt by the side of it, and prayed. She looked up at the stars that showed through her window, now that the rain had ceased.

"And I'm so sorry God, I'm so sorry that I forgot Ruth, that I'll punish myself. I won't go to see Jose today. I promised to, God, and maybe he'll expect me, but I'll punish myself. Dear God, please make him miss me. . . ."

CHAPTER XIII

A LITTLE DISCOVERY

"You see," said Mr. Aguilar, there on the hilltop with Pollyanna and Jimmy, "it was my great-uncle who sold that mine to Mr. Aguamonte. That's why I am on the track of the same thing. Oh, but don't misunderstand me. I'm not after gold. I'm not even after the mine. I'm looking for something else, but the mine, I thought, would lead me to it. So you see, if you'll trust me, I think we could work together."

"What is it you're after?" asked Jimmy directly.

"A lost race," answered Aguilar simply.

He answered the inquiring, interested look in both faces.

"I'll tell you," he said. "It's a bit of a secret, because if I am on the track of anything, I'd rather like the credit for what I find, but if you are not archæologists, it won't make any difference to you. Especially if you promise to keep silent."

"But I thought you were a lawyer," put in Pollyanna.

"That's how I earn my living, such as it is," he

answered. "But this sort of thing . . . digging, adventuring . . . treasure hunts that yield results for posterity and history rather than just wealth for one man or a few . . . this is what I live by."

"Miss Aguamonte gave me to understand that the whole transaction about the mine was something of a gentleman's agreement," said Jimmy slowly. "Mr. Aguamonte regarded it less of a sale than a loan, and on that basis, he never worked the mine himself, until the man who sold it to him had died, and his own children and family needed money. So. . . ."

"As a lawyer, in settling some affairs for my family, I had occasion to go through all my Uncle's papers," said the young man, "even his private correspondence. I found his correspondence with Mr. Aguamonte, and also some private notes of his own that he had made, and among his things a small trinket or two, labeled from 'within the mine,' and that's how I started thinking about the place.

"In occasional weeks off from the office in Mexico City, I have come here, with supplies enough for a day or two, and a shovel. I naturally haven't the faintest thought of interfering in any way with Miss Aguamonte's rights, and I have every reason to want to help you find that mine.

"Have you thought about the shape of this mountain—the look of that plain there below?"

"Why," said Pollyanna, wonderingly, "I hadn't

noticed before, but it looks almost square, doesn't
it?"

The valley was indeed of a regular shape, with
almost straight sides, and each side, as marked out by
the foot of a peak, almost as long as the others.

"That's so," said Jimmy. "And it measures almost square, too, as a matter of fact."

"Doesn't that indicate anything to you?" Mr.
Aguilar's eyes were shining behind his glasses; his
face was eager and excited as a child's.

"Not specially," said Jimmy slowly. "You mean,
do I think it might indicate that the valley was hand-
made, in a sense. . . . No. I've seen other works of
nature, definitely works of nature, that were start-
ling in their regularity."

"I didn't mean that," said Mr. Aguilar. "But if
you have studied the ancient peoples, those forma-
tions of nature that were striking by their apparent
resemblance to man-made images or thoughts or
things were always noticed, and made the sites of
special ceremonies, or the objects of special interest,
even veneration.

"Many a lovely temple has been built in the midst
of a round valley and many another on top of a
strangely-shaped hill. . . . If you were going to
select a site for a temple, or a fortress, could you

find a better one than this conical mountain, looking down into that squarish valley. . . ."

"But," said Pollyanna gently, "you must have more to go on than imaginative speculations about what you might have done."

"I have those trinkets of my Uncle's," he said. "They are of gold, beautifully carved. Little god-like figures. I took them to the museum, and Mexico's greatest archæologist studied them. He told me that they were undoubtedly very old, perhaps dating to a time when the Mayans flourished, but that he could not place them exactly, nor definitely connect them with any of the civilizations known to students of ancient Mexico. He advised me to hunt further for them, or for bones, or stones . . . or graves. . . ."

Pollyanna dropped her eyes along the mountain-side to where Mr. Aguilar had been working about the caves on the other side of the valley.

"Did you think that those caves might contain tombs, then?" she asked.

"They seemed to be a good place to begin to look," he said. "But I didn't find much. Just a few bones. They were not specially old bones. I took them to Mexico City, and they yielded no results . . . except that I was told that they were of no value at all."

"Well then," said Jimmy, "you are in the same boat we are. You know that there is something hereabouts that you want to find. But there are no clues, and therefore all you've got to go on is sheer luck, and hunches."

"That's it. I came up here today, just on a hunch. I noticed from the valley floor that right here was where the first rays of the sun fell in the morning. That might have a significance. But so far . . . nothing."

"Your hunch is as good as mine," said Jimmy. "I'll tell you. I have a hunch that that lake down there is full of secrets."

"What makes you think so?"

"Because of some things Miss Aguamonte told me. You see, she received word that her father was killed in the mine . . . drowned. Some underground stream, from within the mountain burst out into the tunnels and flooded them . . . or something like that. The only news she ever got came from some Indians, and they may have garbled it a bit in their fright. You've noticed that they are afraid of the place."

"Yes. That's true."

"So I proceeded on the notion that the stream probably might wash out of the mountain at the old mine entrance. But there is no such stream. There must have been a quake since then, changing everything, perhaps burying our mine, and your treasures, irrevocably."

"I hope not." Mr. Aguilar's words were like a prayer.

"The only thing," said Jimmy, "is the lake. It is fed from below, evidently. I thought it might be by a spring. But it is just barely possible—there is a chance—that it may be fed by an underground stream. . . ."

"It's possible . . ." breathed Mr. Aguilar.

"It's icy cold water. I don't think I could explore it myself. We'll have to rig up some sort of diving bell or something, I guess."

Mr. Aguilar turned toward him impulsively.

"Let's work together!"

"You bet!" said Jimmy, and they shook hands gravely.

"Well," said Pollyanna, "then the next thing for us to do is to go back to civilization and get the proper materials for further work, and bring them in here. Isn't it?"

"Yes."

"So we had better get back down to camp, and start as soon as possible. You'll eat with us, Mr. Aguilar."

"Thank you. I have my Ford parked in the village, down on the other side of the mountain. If you don't mind being crowded in with some equipment, we can drive back to Mexico City together."

"Splendid."

They started down the ridge of the mountain soberly, choosing their steps with care, for though the slope was not steep, the fall down would have been long, and there were rough rocks to make it dangerous.

Pollyanna stopped suddenly, on the way down, and cried, "Look Jimmy!"

"Where?"

"Over there. Look at those rocks."

"By George."

And Mr. Aguilar, without speaking, began to scramble over the ridge toward a flat place on the one across the ravine, where Pollyanna pointed. Pollyanna and Jimmy followed eagerly, but slowly.

"It's wonderful!" cried Aguilar. "Look!"

And what Pollyanna had seen from the opposite ridge lay before them,—the tips of what seemed to be rings of rocks, set in semi-circles, flat-topped rocks, as if they may have been seats. And in the center a great square one, half-buried in soil.

"Ah, this was done by man," cried Aguilar. "These stones were set out so by man. They didn't just happen! We have something! Thank you, Mrs. Pendleton!"

"It is strange, isn't it," breathed Pollyanna, standing near the great central rock, and looking out across the valley, "how from here you would look straight across the top of the mountain opposite, and probably straight into the dying sun. Maybe they built fires on the top of the other mountain."

"We'll go and see!" Mr. Aguilar was shoveling away the dirt as fast as he could from the stone tips that protruded through the soil. Panting and heaving, he was working passionately, laughing.

"Here. Let me spell you."

Jimmy took the shovel from him, and began to dig around the stones too.

In a little while they had cleared away the earth from one of the stones, and it stuck out of the ground, nicely squared, like a bench.

And then Jimmy's shovel struck something ringing.

"Hold on," he yelled, like a boy at a football game. "There's something down here! A kind of floor!"

"Give it to me!" Mr. Aguilar snatched the shovel, and began working furiously.

"I wish I could help," cried Pollyanna. "It's so exciting!"

Taking turns one after the other, laughing and

grunting a bit at the effort, for it was not easy work, they labored away, and at the end of an hour, they began to see what they had found.

It was a row of seats, arranged semi-circularly, set on a sort of paved platform. In the middle was the big square stone, that must have been where the important ones in the discussion, whoever they might be, sat in state.

"But this may not be so very old," put in Pollyanna, suddenly. "As old as the little gold things, that you found in your Uncle's things, I mean."

"That's true," said Aguilar, who was resting a moment. "But it is something, and it is interesting in itself. It will make this trip seem less unproductive, at any rate."

Pollyanna shaded her eyes and looked across at the ridge where they had met Aguilar that morning.

"Do you know," she said suddenly, "this place is on a direct line with where you were working. A direct line in relation to the sun. I imagine that the sun would strike here, first thing after it rose, too."

"I think you are right," he said.

Jimmy was digging furiously around the great square slab of stone in the center. After some time, he stood back, and said, "Aguilar, look. We shall have to cover this over again."

"Paintings!"

Along the side of the stone bench, in little squares, one beside another, were small designs, somewhat faded, but still apparent. The colors were dull blue, a sort of reddish rust, and bright yellow, and white.

"This is a marvelous find! And we owe it to your sharp eyes, Mrs. Pendleton."

"Can you tell about what period it came from?" asked Pollyanna.

"I should say . . ." he studied a while. "I think it must be Aztec or Toltec. I don't think it is from one of the more ancient kingdoms. But I don't pretend to be an authority. I must bring one of the best archæologists up here. The government will want to know about this.

"But I am hopeful," he said. "You know, just as the excavators who found the ancient Troy discovered that seven other cities had been built above it, and had been plowed under by the sand of years, so we often find more ancient monuments still under the ancient Aztec ones. The same natural sites that one people will choose for a city or a temple, are likely to appeal to the next race, hundred and thousands of years later. And then, you know, it has always been the custom of man, the world over, when he conquers a people, to set up his own gods and heroes where the conquered ones used to reign."

"I suggest," said Pollyanna, drawing some chocolate out of her jacket pockets, "that we refresh ourselves, and that we then go back down to the valley, really eat something, and then break camp. You'll have to get equipment and men to begin the work you see ahead. You'll have to have an artist make sketches of these things, won't you? . . ."

"And I shall want a good photographer," said Aguilar.

"And we've lots to do."

"And," said Jimmy, "you've been thinking of your children all morning, and you're eager to start back home. Aren't you?"

"Yes," confessed Pollyanna. "I have loved it here—really—but I would like to get back to the children. I'm really a home body—I don't belong with you two adventurers!

"And I'm worried about Nancy," she concluded suddenly, turning to Jimmy. "She's so stubborn. She's so likely to disobey the doctor and get out of bed, and overdo."

"Mrs. Pendleton is speaking of Nancy, our children's nurse," Jimmy explained to Mr. Aguilar. "She was my wife's nurse too, when she was little, but Nancy thinks she's as young and strong as she used to be. She isn't of course. And she's not well. She has to rest in bed for a while."

"I should think," said Mr. Aguilar, looking at his watch, "that we might be able to pack up and start back today. We'd get into the village at night, but we could sleep there, and then make an early morning start in the Ford."

They covered over the precious bits of old painting with earth again, so that rain and sun might not fade it, and then, shouldering the shovel, Jimmy led the way down to camp.

Mr. Aguilar went across the valley to get what little gear he had brought, and Pollyanna gave orders for a meal, and then packing.

One of the Indians began immediately to take down the tiny tent, and to rope things together to pack on one of the donkeys.

When Mr. Aguilar got back, with his blankets tied up and slung across his shoulders, the hot meal of beans was ready. Beans and bread and coffee, and cheese.

It was about three in the afternoon when they set out along the trail they had come.

Pollyanna began to sing to herself, some wordless little song, and Mr. Aguilar smiled at her understandingly.

"We are all happy," he said.

CHAPTER XIV

JUNIOR'S SECRET, AND THE ART SCHOOL

MRS. MORENO sat in Pollyanna's patio and sipped her tea. Her little girl, Anita, about as tall as Ruth, but slim, and brown, though her hair was as golden as Ruth's, sat beside Ruth under a rose bush, and solemnly they turned the pages of a big book together.

"I am glad your husband will go with mine along the road again, to Monterey," she said. "They are such friends. Ramon thinks everything of Mr. Pendleton."

"Jimmy wants to have a long talk with Miss Aguamonte," said Pollyanna. "It's possible that the government may help finance the exploration of the mountain where her mine is. But it's also possible that the government may take over some of the mine in the interests of Mexican archæology and history. Don't say anything about this—it's confidential. But as I know Jimmy will take your husband into his confidence, I might as well tell you. There may be some wonderful discoveries there in that mine!"

146

"Gold and diamonds?" asked Ruth suddenly, and as the two women turned and looked at the two intent little faces under the rose bush, they realized that the book on the two brown pairs of knees had not been interesting them as much as the conversation.

"Ruthie," said Pollyanna. "You ask Judy to take you and Anita over to see Jose in the church tower where the bells are. Maybe Jose will play Anita a tune on the bells."

"All right, Mama."

And Ruth took Anita by the hand and went to find Judy.

But Mrs. Moreno had not put down her cup of tea, when Ruth came back, still holding fast to Anita's hand, and reported, "Judy's on her bed, crying, Mama. And when I said, 'What for' she said 'Go away.' "

"Well, go into the kitchen to see Lolita then, and ask her to show you how to make something. Something that Anita would like."

"Can I ask her to make chocolate, Mama?"

"Yes."

The children pattered away into the kitchen, and presently they could hear Lolita's voice, and the clatter of pans.

"Will you go back again to the mine with your

husband? I think you were very brave to go. I almost never go with Ramon on his rough trips. I am afraid."

"No, you're not afraid," said Pollyanna. "You just prefer not to, isn't that so?"

"Well, yes," said Mrs. Moreno, laughing. "I don't look very nice in hiking clothes."

"I am sure you would look nice in anything," said Pollyanna. "But I don't think I shall go again. Not soon, anyway." She lowered her voice. "I am worried about Nancy. Our nurse. She is like one of the family. Very dear to us. And she is quite ill. More ill than we let her know.

"She was ordered to bed to rest, but she got up and went out in the rain, while Ruth was lost—it was while I was away—and she had a severe chest cold following that. She is just getting better. But I can't leave her again, until she is really well."

"Of course not," said Mrs. Moreno. "Well, if you are going to be in town regularly then, you might like to come with me to some exhibits and even to the art class. I began taking some lessons recently, and the teacher encourages me. Would you like to?"

"I'd love to," said Pollyanna.

There was a knock at the front door, and after a moment Lolita emerged from the kitchen, walking

swiftly and silently in her sandals, to open it.   At
the same moment Judy flashed out of her bedroom,
and stood waiting expectantly, tears drying on her
flushed cheeks, and her dark hair in disorder.

"Come in," said Lolita, and Jose stepped into the
hallway, hatless.

"But I thought you had forgotten!" cried Judy,
all smiles, running toward him.

"I am late," said Jose, "but I have not forgotten."

"Mother," Judy led Jose into the patio and pre-
sented him, proudly, to her mother and Mrs. Moreno.
"Jose and I were going to go over to the school
gymnasium and watch the basketball game. I was
afraid he had forgotten." Her starry eyes were
bright with eagerness now. She hadn't the slight-
est idea that her mother might say "no."

"You may go," said Pollyanna kindly, "if Junior
goes with you."

"But he isn't here." Judy's face fell, and her
eyes clouded.

"Then wait for him," suggested Pollyanna. "He
won't be long, surely. Ruthie and Anita are learning how to make chocolate in the kitchen. Perhaps
they'll give you some."

"I'll tell you," suggested Jose, "I'll go out to look
for Junior. I think he'd like to come."

"All right." Judy accompanied him to the door.

Mrs. Moreno smiled significantly ab
"The first little love affair?" she asked

"They begin at about this age, I think
anna, a little uneasily.

"These little affections are easily ma
Mrs. Moreno. "They come this way
dreaming over books. He seems like
boy."

"I am sure of it," said Pollyanna.
is a strange child, high-strung, imag i
idealistic. She was very happy having
sons in California, and was doing well
I had better find her something to do."

"What about the art classes that I ta
are children in the school. Why don
take lessons. I should think she might
painting or sketching."

"I think you're right," said Pollyann
bring her with me and come with you so
when you are going to the classes?"

"Of course. Tomorrow if you like."

"Tomorrow would be splendid."

* * * * * * *

Junior had a real secret. A secret he
with only one person . . . Jose.

That year in Hollywood, the close frie

Happy Banks, the cinema's greatest silent comedian, and the tutoring he had had in camera tricks under Happy's photographers, had taught rather a special lot about photography for a young lad. And it was a genuine passion with him. Another California friend of his, Charlie Wing, a Chinese, and also a camera addict, had strengthened his natural good taste, and had much influenced his sense of proportion and of simplification. He had made some really good studies. Now he had determined to enter a contest,—a camera contest he had read about.

Choice of subject matter was to be one of the qualities judged in the pictures submitted.

"That's why," he had confided to Jose, "I hope to take a prize. Of course, technically I can't compete with the great entrants like Steichen and Beaton and some of the Japanese photographers, but with these lovely scenes to choose from . . . I don't see how I can help being noticed! Will you help me? Come with me, I mean, and talk Spanish with people so that they'll pose, and let me photograph their donkeys and things. I want to have people in every picture. . . ."

All this was worked out in several long sessions, for Jose's English failed him at crucial moments, as did Junior's Spanish. But they wanted to understand each other, and that helped very much.

One of the first sets of pictures Junior took was

studies in the belfry and from it, looking toward
Mexico City.

He had one of Jose's father at the bells, with the
thick late afternoon sun making a blur of light around
him and the bells, that he counted much on.   There
was another one of Jose, quickly snapped, even before Jose was aware of it, which showed him standing pointing toward the plaza, his brown boyish face
animated, the wind in his curling dark hair, and a
bird wheeling in the sky not far behind him.

Then there was another picture, a picture Junior
was setting his hopes on.   It had been taken a. the
bullfight.

Pollyanna did not know he had gone.   It was not
a real bullfight.   It was a corrida for "aficionados,"
or amateurs.   Junior, despite manly affectations,
was soft-hearted.   He couldn't watch the ring itself.
He watched the audience, and he had his camera
ready, already focused in the shade of the best seats.
He had taken some distance snaps of the Queens of
the Bullfight—pretty girls with dark shining eyes and
wide flashing smiles, their dark hair covered with
darker lace propped high against towering combs,
and with flowers tucked in among the folds of lace.

Then there was a shout!   Junior looked down,
inadvertently into the ring.   A bull was sinking to

its knees, the handle of a bright sword protruding
from its back.   Beside him, poised on slender feet,
stood the matador, his red cape over his arm.

But Junior saw this only for a flash, only momen-
tarily.   What delighted him was the sudden rain of
whirling straw hats, as the delighted audience threw
them down into the ring, to indicate their pleasure.
The air was full of the yellow whirling straw hats,
and the people were on their feet, shouting and excited.   Junior got a picture, from way above, of
those hats, like a cloud of sunflowers, whirling downward toward the sand, where the dying animal col-
lapsed on its knees.

Today, while Pollyanna and Mrs. Moreno took
tea in the patio, he was out wandering about among
the markets, his camera in its leather case slung
across his shoulders.

He had taken one picture. An old woman, wrapped
in her black rebosa, crouched by her little store of
bananas, which were laid out on a dark brown cloth
on the pavement.   She was old as the hills; her
wrinkles showed deep as cuts in her dark face. With
one hand she held her rebosa around her face, shading her eyes from the sun, and with the other she
cooked her bit of hot lunch on a charcoal brazier by
her side.   The change from her sales lay, silver and

copper, on her black skirt, where her old eyes could easily find the coins in making change for another customer.

He was getting ready to try to photograph a little laden donkey, waiting patiently outside a pulqueria, or pulque saloon, which was labeled "My Office," no doubt in order to confuse and amuse. He wanted to get it against the sun, outlined in a soft golden glow.

But just then Jose laid his hand on his arm.

"Hola!"

"Hola, amigo."

"Will you come to the basketball game in the school gymnasium? It has already begun, but it is good fun, and free. They will play for championships next month, and they are good at the game."

"Yes, I'd like to, Jose."

"Come then. The little sister wishes also to go."

"Judy?"

"Yes."

"Now I see why you asked me. Mama wouldn't let her go without me." Junior was awkwardly teasing in his tone, but he felt a little prick of hurt at being asked so late.

"I wanted you to come all the time," said Jose. "I asked Judy to ask you, yesterday. But she says she forgot."

"Well, then . . ." Junior was a little mollified.

"Say," he said, after a minute. "You know, I think Judy's kind of stuck on you."

Jose said nothing, but his color rose.

"She keeps dressing up all the time, and she certainly does act funny."

But Jose threw a comradely arm across Junior's shoulders, and dismissed the matter.

"She's just a girl," he said. And they called at the house and matter-of-factly took the trembling and delighted Judy to the game, treating her with manly frankness.

So that she wept because of a sort of unexplained, inexplicable sense of disappointment. She had been at the ball game with Jose. But it was as nothing. He and Junior had talked all the time, and neither one had paid much attention to her.

* * * * * * *

The art classes were very unlike anything Pollyanna had ever seen or expected. In the first place, they were conducted in one of the oldest and most beautiful buildings in Mexico City,—in a palace that had housed a vice-roy. Once inside the great entrance gates, which were made of wood, studded with great square-tipped coarse nails, they stepped into a

flagged court, as large as half a city block in the
United States. The building towered to the sky
in three stories, with high-ceilinged rooms opening
onto balconies, and the balconies were arched and
beautiful, open to the sun and air.

In the open flagged court there were plaster casts
of some Greek statues, famous the world over as the
first sketching material for young artists, and there
were also many stone and plaster images of Mexican
gods and goddesses, centuries old, with strange large-
featured yet Oriental faces, and elaborate head-
dresses.

Easels stood about, and children and older people
were working away, oblivious to those who entered
and looked.

A tall stout man moved among the easels, suggest-
ing here, adding a few strokes there.

"That is one of Mexico's greatest painters," whispered Mrs. Moreno to Pollyanna. "He comes to
contribute his services, criticising and teaching, as
often as he can. But he is terribly busy, and can't
get in as much as he would like to."

They went up the broad noble flight of stairs. On
the balconies of the second floor, with an old man
from the street as model, students were working at
quick sketching in color.

"Some of the life classes, and lectures, and studies

in anatomy are held in the rooms that open off this balcony," explained Mrs. Moreno. "My class in oil sketching is usually over there, in one of those rooms. Today we are going to work outside, though."

"What's up there?" Judy was pointing to the third floor.

"The modeling is done up there. Are you interested in modeling?"

"May we see it?"

"Of course."

The balconies on the third floor were filled with casts of birds, animals, and god-like creatures. Students in white blouses stood over heaps of greenish clay on tables in the inside rooms.

Judy said nothing as she was led through these rooms, and watched the students at work.

Before a statuette of a dancer, light as the wind, every muscle showing grace and balance and strength, Judy paused, fascinated.

"I love that," she said simply. "Isn't that beautiful, Mother?"

Pollyanna looked at the nymphlike, flying figure, and thought it of rather a sentimental grace at first, —unreal. But then she saw it with the eyes of her twelve-year-old daughter, awakening to beauty, but still with eyes that could see little but dreams, ideals,

hopes. . . .   Even earthly loveliness would be to her,
for some years still, entwined in the mists of poetry,
not seen for its coverings. . . .

"It's lovely, Judy," she said.   "Would you like to
study modeling, do you think?   I could arrange for
you to study here, I believe."

"Oh, Mother. . . .   If you'd only. . . .   I'd be so
happy."

CHAPTER XV

THE FIRST "ADIOS"

EARLY one morning, about two weeks later, Pollyanna woke the children herself. It was a bright day, sunny and warm. Already the long fingers of the early light crept in underneath the closed shutters, and trembled across the dark tiled floor.

"Come Ruthie," she whispered. "Get up quietly. Get dressed by yourself, darling, but mama will come in to button you in back, and to help you with the shoes."

"What for, Mama? Isn't this early?" Ruth's warm little peach-glow cheek cuddled into the curve of Pollyanna's neck, and her sleepy eyes closed again.

Pollyanna shook her gently.

"You're going on a surprise party, darling. All day."

"All right, Mama."

Pollyanna went to the other side of the bed.

"Judy. . . ."

"Um . . . ?"

"Judy, get up now."

"Aaaaw, Mama!" protestingly, but sweetly. Judy looked lovely in the morning, with the warm color of sleep in her cheeks, her violet eyes dark, her hair touseled and curly.

"A surprise party. You're going on a big picnic with Mrs. Moreno and some other children. She's giving you all breakfast at her house first."

Ruth paused in the act of pulling her nightgown off. Her small face looked through it eagerly.

"A Mexican breakfast? With chocolate?"

"Lots of sweet chocolate," promised Pollyanna.

"Why so early Mother?" Judy was perplexed.

"It's quite late, really. After you have got there, and had your breakfast, you'll be making a late start."

Junior lay in his bed in a rough heap, with bed clothes wound around him, and some on the floor. He had had active dreams.

"Junior! Get up now."

It took ten minutes to get Junior into a state of mind in which he was even awake enough to understand what was being said to him.

"Mrs. Moreno has planned a picnic for you, and you're going to have breakfast in her house first."

"You forgot to tell us yesterday."

"Yes, I'm afraid I did."

"Are you coming?"

"No."

"Why not?"

"Because your father may get home today. I expect him. I'll want him to find me here."

"But I'd like to be home when he gets here, too. Why are you sending us away, Mother? What has happened?"

"Hush. Don't make a noise. I'll tell you, but you must promise not to let Judy or Ruth suspect."

"It's Nancy."

"Yes. Nancy's very very ill. The doctor says today may mean all the difference. We must have absolute quiet."

"All right, Mother. You can trust me."

"I know it, darling." Pollyanna kissed him. He was more like Jimmy every day, manly, honest, and sweet.

Nancy's door was closed as the three children came out into the hall, with their hats and coats on, ready to go.

"Have you got clean handkerchiefs?"

Pollyanna inspected each, smoothed Ruth's hair, tucked in Judy's collar.

"May I say Goodbye to Nancy?" asked Judy suddenly.

"No," answered Pollyanna quickly. "She's asleep."

Judy paled and looked at her mother fixedly. But

then she turned, took Ruth's hand, and silently went toward the door.

"The automobile is waiting for you outside," said Pollyanna. "The man will take you straight to Mrs. Moreno's house. Junior, look after your little sisters."

"I will, mother."

All three kissed her goodbye. The door closed behind them. Pollyanna heard the sound of the motor as the automobile pulled away from in front of the house and went down the road.

Then she went blindly over to a seat in the patio, and sat there weeping, like a child, sobbing and crying, with the tears rolling down her cheeks un- mopped and unnoticed.

She sat there a long time, thinking, and weeping, while the sun crept up into the sky. Then she closed her eyes and made a little prayer, and tried to compose herself. She smoothed back her yellow hair, dried her eyes, sat very still.

The bells from the cathedral sounded, loud and deep, and slow.

All around her were living things—flowers, in- sects, little birds wheeling in the sky. But Nancy slept unheeding.

Finally Pollyanna rose and went into Nancy's room with a quick step. She straightened the covers

on the bed, smoothed the gray hair off Nancy's forehead. Nancy lay very still, very still. There was a
little smile on her lips, and her tired eyes were closed.
She looked happy.

It was Lolita standing hovering in the doorway,
her face compassionate, her eyes understanding.

"It is the doctor, Mrs. Pendleton. He is the one
who must write the paper."

"I'll come at once," said Pollyanna, and, composed
and quiet, she went quickly into the hall where the
doctor waited.

"I shall have to ask a few questions," he said
kindly. "First. . . ."

"In here, doctor."

Pollyanna led the way. As the doctor came into
Nancy's room, she threw open the shutters. The
bright new day streamed in.

The little doctor was quick and silent. He made
his examination deftly. Then he tenderly drew up a
sheet, and covered Nancy's face.

"Rest in peace," he said, and crossed himself.

Pollyanna followed him out into the hall again.

"Let us sit here in the sunlight," she said. "In
the patio."

There Pollyanna answered the questions that were
necessary, and the little doctor wrote down her
answers gravely, in a pretty slanting hand.

"Would you take a cup of coffee with me, doctor?" asked Pollyanna suddenly. "I feel so weak . . . my husband is expected back today . . . but I am lonely here, and I cannot eat alone, or do anything but cry. . . ."

"It would be a pleasure."

Pollyanna called Lolita, and asked her to serve coffee, fruit and hot rolls.

"I have been up all night, doctor, arranging to send the children away, . . . and feeling miserable, of course. She was my childhood nurse, and my children's nurse. They will be heartbroken too. . . ."

"But God, who gives, must take away," he said. He put his little black bag by the side of his chair. "You must think only of those who need you. You must eat and keep strong. God gives us our duties to perform, and when we have finished, he brings us Home."

"You are a religious man, doctor."

"All doctors are, I think. One works with God every moment, healing, bringing life, watching death. I am always close to God."

"I suppose we all are," said Pollyanna, "but we do not remember it."

"Yes," he said gravely.

Lolita had spread a little table, and there in the sunlight, with the flowers and birds around, and the grave little doctor sipping coffee by her side, Pollyanna felt suddenly comforted.

"I can see," he said suddenly, "that your sorrow has lost its edge a little now. You accept God, and God's will,—for a while you resented it. It is the resentment against God's will which gives us pain. When that is gone, then we can only rejoice that God had brought a dear servant Home."

Pollyanna turned to him impulsively, sweetly.

"How good you are!" she said. "You have helped me so much. I will put that on her grave, what you just said. 'God brings his dear servant Home.'"

"It is you who are good," said he, and they ate a bit, companionably.

Then, very quickly, he picked up his bag, and made his farewells.

"Goodbye."

"God be with you."

* * * * * * *

Jimmy arrived at four that afternoon.

By the way Pollyanna clung to him, her quick flooding tears at the sight of him again, he knew.

"Has it happened?" he asked softly, even as he held her.

"Yes. Last night."

"The children . . . ?"

"They're with Mrs. Moreno. She was so sweet.
She promised to keep them a few days. Till it's
over."

"Poor darling. I wish I had been here."

"You're here now, Jimmy."

* * * * * * *

They had the funeral the next day. There is a
little chapel in the cemetery. A protestant minister
read the service for the dead. Jimmy and Pollyanna were the only mourners.

The grave lay under a spreading tree, and from
underneath it Pollyanna, by raising her eyes, could
see the high towering mountains, clouded in mist.

As they turned to go away, she clung tight to
Jimmy's arm.

"It seems so sad that she had to go here . . . in a
strange country . . . away from all her friends. . . ."

"But she was with you, dearest. You know that
is all she would have wished."

* * * * * * *

Lolita met them at the door with a bright smile.
"I have cooked chicken," she said, "and a cho

colate dulce for the little ones. They come back soon. I have word from Mrs. Moreno."

The little house looked the same. Lolita had freshly washed the tiles, and everything was dusted. Candles burned in the little colored glass cups along niches in the walls of the hallway, and the freshly watered flowers in the patio shook off trembling drops, and smelled very sweet. Only Nancy's door was closed and locked.

The knocker sounded, and Pollyanna ran to answer the door. It was Mrs. Moreno and Anita, and Pollyanna's three. Junior and Ruth looked smiling and well. Only Judy was pale and listless.

As the children ran to greet their father Mrs. Moreno said, "The little Judy would not eat. Did she know?"

"No," said Pollyanna. But even as she said it, she saw Judy trying the handle on Nancy's door, and when she found it locked, she turned on her mother a look of agony.

"Mother!"

Pollyanna ran to her and gathered her close in her arms and rocked her.

"Darling, darling, don't cry so. . . ."

"I knew it all the time! I knew it when you said not to say goodbye. . . . Oh, Mother. Mother. It's all my fault. . . ." Her sobs were frightening. The other two children turned to their father with scared eyes, and Pollyanna led the shaking Judy into her bedroom and gently closed the door behind them.

"Oh Mother." Judy flung herself on her knees and hid her face in Pollyanna's lap.

"I did it to her. Because I love Jose. I made her die."

"Come darling. That's impossible. Tell me what you mean." Pollyanna smoothed the rough curls, patted the thin heaving shoulders.

"I love Jose. I just love him. I was up there in the belfry with him, listening to him play, . . . and Ruth was down in the church garden, I thought . . . I should have looked. . . . But I forgot her. . . . I didn't think of her at all until it was dark and I had to go home. . . . You were up at the mine with Daddy. . . . And Ruth was lost. . . . It was raining, Mother . . . pretty hard . . . and everyone was so worried. . . . Lolita went out to get the police . . . and Junior went looking. . . . And Nancy. . . ."

Long sobs here. Judy would be ill, thought Pollyanna unhappily.

"Nancy got up. . . . I begged her not to. . . . And went out in the rain . . . looking. . . ."

Pollyanna took the little girl up in her arms, and rocked her until the sobs quieted at last.

"It's all right, darling. We all forget. Never

mind. The doctor said Nancy died happily in her
sleep. Gently and nicely. While she was dreaming.
She was all well again, my darling. Just terribly
tired. God took her back to him, to rest. . . . Don't
cry, darling."

It was an hour before she left the room. Judy
was tucked into her bed, sleeping exhaustedly, tears
still wet on her pale cheeks.

"Well?" Jimmy was worried.

"She'll be all right," whispered Pollyanna. "Poor
child. She has learned what it means to feel re-
sponsibility. I hope all the other lessons won't come
so hard. . . ."

CHAPTER XVI

IN THE CONVENT GARDEN AT ACTOPAN

THE art classes were going to do something unusual. They were going out into the country, in groups, to visit rural schools. The instructor had explained about it carefully.

"The School of Education has arranged an interesting excursion for all who wish to attend," he had said. "I advise you all, Mexicans and visitors, to go, because you will see Indian groups in their villages responding to education, you will see their native crafts and art work blossoming under helpful guidance, and if you are good at sketching or have vivid memories, you will take away material,— colors—faces—scenes—that you will never forget.

"There will be several excursions. All those who wish to come will sign. There will be only about ten to a group.

"If you like, I will advise about which excursion to choose. But of course you must also put down second and third choices.

"Beginners will go in some groups, experienced sketch workers in another, and so on."

Mrs. Moreno had telephoned Pollyanna about it shortly after her lesson, when the proposed expeditions were announced.

"If you would like to go, I believe I can arrange to join one of the expeditions in my own car, and take you and Judy," she said. "Judy would enjoy it, I know, and you would be awfully interested. Would you like to?"

Pollyanna was eager, but she restrained herself.

"I'll call you later," she promised. "Jimmy is off to the mine for a long stay, recruiting men and so on, very soon. Miss Aguamonte wants to work to get ahead immediately, and he has a partner working with him now. A Mr. Aguilar. Jimmy may take Junior with him. The boy is dying to go. He adores his father, and likes roughing it. And the men think he may be useful with his camera. He's quite good with it. I'll be busy getting them off.

"I'll call you back in plenty of time."

That afternoon, when she took Judy to the art school for her third lesson in modeling—the child was not skilful, but deeply interested—she talked about the excursions with one of the art teachers, Señor Torres.

"Do you know anything about our rural schools, Mrs. Pendleton?"

"I'm ashamed to say that I don't."

"Well, I may tell you something about them, then, since my sister has majored in education at the university, and she is very enthusiastic about the work.

"We in Mexico have a different education problem from yours in the states. There are many parts of Mexico in which Spanish is not understood. There are still many parts where the population is pure Indian, where for centuries there has been no change in methods of living, agriculture, housing, or anything. It has been only since the partition of the lands—a move that worked some hardships of course, but we all hope and believe it was for the best—that the rural schools have come into existence as they are now operated.

"For some time the education department had to convince the bulk of the Mexicans that the Indians were capable of profiting by schools. The first thing they did was start a normal school here in Mexico City, to educate the Indians so that they might in turn educate others. They brought Indians from every section of Mexico and put them in school, and definitely proved that they were of high capacity and ambition. But they didn't all of them want to return to the backward sections and teach. Some of them, many of them, wanted to remain here.

"So a new plan was started. Schools were started, in all the remote districts not served by local schools and the Indians were taught Spanish, reading, writing, useful arithmetic, history, domestic sciences, hygiene, and improved agriculture—but they were not things that they could not do by themselves, without involving themselves in hopeless debts for machines or instruments. Scientific farmers were able to teach them a good deal about how to work their land more profitably, though, without spending money, and the women took to the domestic teaching and hygiene very well. Then, within those very schools, teachers were trained to carry on the work, and the school was left in their hands, while the original teachers went on to some other district to start the same work again.

"Then besides, the education department sends around buses, once or twice, or more often, every year, to take plays, and books, and music, and movies to the outlying districts. . . ."

"How wonderful!" Pollyanna meant it.

"They have something like eight thousand of those rural schools now," he said, "maybe more. They are building more all the time. The teachers begin their work in any little building, hastily erected. They do not compel attendance. They just wait, teaching whoever they can, until the people ask for the education. The government believes that people appreciate most and profit most by what they desire. After the people are convinced, and come to the school, and one leader or more among their group is trained to continue the work, with constant help from the central department of education——they usually get together and build schoolhouses, and generally cooperate to the extent of making the school the center of their cultural and civic life."

The young man was enthusiastic, and Pollyanna caught it from his words and his expression.

"It's a fine work," she said. "Very fine and understanding. I should love to visit one of the schools."

Judy, who loved any sort of expedition into the country, decided that she would like nothing better than to go, too.

So Pollyanna decided to call Mrs. Moreno after dinner that very evening, and make plans to go and see a real rural school for herself.

After the art class was over, and Judy had proudly packed away a small shaky but recognizable figure of a dog, modeled in green clay, that she wanted her father to see, Pollyanna and Judy walked along the narrow streets, lined with beautiful old colonial buildings, now turned into shops, and past the most modern of fine business buildings and shops, on wide paved streets, for Mexico is a city of contrasts, where one may find almost anything he has eyes to look for. They walked along the central square, onto which look the handsome long red buildings of the Governor's palace, and the dignified and lovely cathedral, tall and brown against the blue sky.

Pollyanna had a few purchases to make in the shops along the other side of the square, opposite the palace. Then she and Judy got into a taxi—taxis are very cheap and reliable in Mexico City, and Jimmy had instructed her to use them often—and gave the address of their little pink house in the suburbs.

As they drew up they saw Jimmy himself, out in front, in the hot sunshine, loading a car with gear.

"They're getting ready to go," she said to Judy, with that catch in the throat that she always felt, no matter how frequent their separations.

After she had paid and dismissed the taxi man Pollyanna sent Judy into the house while she walked over to where Jimmy was heaving still one more package into the tonneau of the car.

"Hello dear!"

"Hello! I'll be through here in a minute, honey. Then I'll be in to wash up and tell you our plans. We're starting early tomorrow for the big push."

"The big push?"

"We'll be gone a long time. I've orders to find something, and to stay till I do."

"Would you like dinner early?"

"Yes, I would. We'll be turning in early, Junior and I, because we're to start very early. About four. Aguilar will come by for us. I already fixed everything with Lolita to be up and give us breakfast here before we start."

Pollyanna's next words were silenced by the cathedral bells, sounding deeply and sweetly and very loud. So she went into the house, and into her room. She took off her hat, and glanced into the mirror, and stood there looking ruefully at her sad face until Jimmy came bursting in, and put his own brown face down close to hers and laughed at their two reflections.

"Why so lorn, Pollyanna?"

"I was just thinking that I was rather a nice person, and kind of pleasant-looking, and it seems too bad that I'm a widow so much."

His face sobered for a moment.

"The hardship is mine, darling."

She pulled herself out of her depressed mood, for

her nature was naturally sunny, and she knew it
was unfair.

"I suppose Junior is beside himself to be taken
along."

"He is. And it'll be great to have him. He'll
learn a lot, and see a lot, and I rather think he'll be
terribly useful. If we really make any discoveries
such as those Aguilar is counting on. . . ."

"And then, of course," said Pollyanna, "there is
that sort of council rock. . . ."

"You bet! Won't let us forget that find of yours,
will you?"

"Certainly not," cried Pollyanna gaily. "I want
it named after me."

"We'll speak to the authorities about it," Jimmy
promised.

* * * * * * *

The evening sped quickly. The departure the
next morning was over soon. The three men—
Pollyanna was beginning to think of Junior as a man
now, as often as she thought of him as a boy—were
off and away, and the house was still and empty.
The two little girls were still in their beds, sound
asleep.

Pollyanna returned to hers, but not to sleep. After

the fashion of mothers, she was going with the absent ones, each step of the journey, timing them, imagining what they were doing now, where they had got to, how they were faring.

But toward eight o'clock, she fell into a drowse, and she was awakened only by the morning sound of the chimes.

Judy was awake too, listening for them. She woke every morning and listened for them.

*   *   *   *   *   *   *

"Where are we going, Mama? What is the name of the place?"

Judy and Pollyanna sat in the back seat, with Mrs. Moreno in between them, and Anita on a small seat let down to make the car six-passenger. The chauffeur shared the front seat with a large package of picnic edibles.

"We are going to Actopan," said Mrs. Moreno. "Actopan is not far away from Pachuca, on the new highway between Mexico City and San Antonio. Soon many tourists will know all about Actopan. There is one of the loveliest of old convents there, and the government is spending a good deal of money peeling down the walls to the original frescoes, which are very beautiful. We shall study them today, and Señor Torres, the teacher of our art class, will tell us about them."

They had left Mexico City now, and the road wound among little foothills, on which the tall, symmetrical maguey grew, bluish green against the sundried brown grass. The arch of sky above was a deep heavenly blue, thick with shining white clouds to the west.

"Are you going to paint today, Mamacita?" This from little Anita, in Spanish.

"No, baby. Today we are just going to listen. and look, and study."

"And eat our picnic," concluded Anita.

"Yes, baby."

Judy kept her eyes on the road, and on the changing countryside. Now they slid along a fair straight highway between tall trees, and now they came out upon a curving blue ribbon of asphalt, smoothly ascending a hillside, with the maguey growing thick on either side, and the bits of earth in between sweet-smelling and bright with yellow flowers.

It was after they had been riding and chatting for about an hour and a half that the chauffeur stopped the car for a moment, and pointed out two tall gray rocks that stood on the top of a nearby hill, silhouetted against the cloudy sky.

"I thought you'd like to catch a good view of 'Los Frailes,' " he said.

"What are they?" asked Pollyanna.

Mrs. Moreno explained.

"Look closely. They look, those two stones, like a monk and a nun, do they not?"

"They do, a bit."

"When we get closer, and have other views, you will see the resemblance better. Well, the Indians of this country tell a legend to explain those stones."

"What is the legend?" begged Judy, with shining eyes.

"I'll tell it to you. Can you see how dry the country is here, how very little is growing but the maguey?"

"Yes."

"There is so little water, you see. Well, there are two great religious houses in this part of the country. Or rather, there were. There was one for nuns, and one for monks, both vowed to live only for God and to devote themselves to His service.

"The Indians tell that there came a very dry year, and the wells in the convent and monastery gardens dried, and there was no water for them. So the nuns sent one of their number barefoot across the hills searching for a spring. And, far away, the monastery sent out a monk, barefooted too, to search for water for them. And while the nun was gone, all the nuns knelt and prayed to God that her search would be rewarded, and in the monastery gardens, the monks also knelt and prayed that the one they had sent forth to search would find water.

"The two searched, and searched, and they could find nothing. In their wanderings they came upon each other. They met there on the mountain top, where you see them now. And they forgot their vows, and those who waited for them, and their search, and they fell in love. But God was angry, and when they exchanged their first kiss, he sent a thunderbolt that brought the rain pouring down from heaven, but they never moved again, for God had turned them into stone. And they have stood ever since."

"Only for a kiss?" murmured Judy.

"It was against their vows."

"Well, there they stand, always together, any-way," said Judy.

"You are a romanticist, little Judy," said Mrs. Moreno, laughing and patting Judy's slender arm.

The chauffeur started the car again, and they climbed up the mountain, and then began a long slow descent, curving along the mountain-side, into a little valley. Twisting and turning, they did not notice that suddenly 'Los Frailes', or 'The Monk and the Nun' stood very much closer, on a neighboring hillside.

"There they are," said Anita suddenly,
a short brown finger.
They all looked again. Yes, they
recognizable. A tall monk, in a hoode
a small and slender nun, her headdress
little in the wind, or so it seemed.
"The Indians in this part of the count
poor," said Mrs. Moreno, and her sweet
clouded a little thinking of it. "You c
some of them live, still." She pointed
hovel made of earth bricks, mud, and
enough to crawl into, when the wind w
the night black.
"They get so little water here, and the
it is good, can yield little without rain
"They live on the maguey. Sometime
no liquid at all to drink but the juice of
. . . and that is terribly strong, very
after it has stood fermenting for some
don't know how to prevent it from
Maybe they don't want to.
"If there is a bit of water, collected in
have to give it to the animals to drink.
are their life—the burros and the magu
"They drink the juice of the mague
the leaves to build their houses, they m
the fiber. . . . It is a very useful plant

Pollyanna looked at some of the miserable little huts and felt sorry.

"Poor things," she said.

"Well," said Mrs. Moreno, "you will see what the school of education is helping to do for these people. We in Mexico interpret education very broadly— or rather we give it a full meaning. Education is teaching people how to make the most of themselves, their environment, and their life.

"The teachers are showing the Indians how, by not much more effort, they may build really comfortable and clean houses, that stand the weather better. They are quick to learn. To some people it may seem as if they improve slowly, but really, to us in Mexico, it seems very remarkable indeed."

The road ran along the plain now. There was a bit of a stream flowing sluggishingly on one side. Little patches of cultivated ground showed green, and they could see the Indians out working, always assisted by the little gray donkeys, with their wise eyes.

The houses seemed better constructed here, and the people they passed in the road seemed well-dressed in coarse clean cottons, well-fed, happy.

"Now we are coming to the town of Actopan," said Mrs. Moreno. A small sign pointed to a side road off the main highway.

They rolled along, looking at the fields of grain,
the haystacks on either side of the road. Suddenly
they came into the little old town,—a very old town
indeed. It had been founded not very long after the
Spanish had conquered the Indians of the country,
and had set up their own Moorish-Gothic Roman
civilization, to mix in with the Aztec and Toltec
civilizations already there in Mexico.

The town is low-lying to the ground, colonial, a
soft dusty pink in color. Around the plaza are a
few little sleepy shops, where groceries and stamps
and refrescos—or soda pop in bottles—are sold. In
the plaza grow some flowers and trees, and there are
benches standing about, and children playing, and
there are many dogs stretched out asleep in the sun,
their tails twitching uneasily in dreams.

A haze of golden-pink seems to lie over the town,
a haze that colors everything divinely, that imparts
a sense of age and ease to the scene, within which
everything moves with a languid grace.

"How beautiful it is!" Pollyanna just breathed
the words.

"It is lovely," agreed Mrs. Moreno. "We must
go on now to the monastery. The party will be
waiting there. And you will find it well worth the
trip, just the monastery itself. I know that."

Sure enough, there were several cars parked outside the high walls of the ancient monastery garden,

and from inside Pollyanna could hear a babble of voices.

They got out of their car and entered the church first. Inside, the cool dark air smote them suddenly, for they were used to the warmth and brightness outside, and they shivered a little. The church was empty. The party had gone on into the gardens.

Far far up into the arched ceiling Judy looked. She fancied she could see the little angel faces painted on the ceiling looking down at her through the films of paint that had been laid on over them, by well-meaning people. But there were already workmen busy with little chisels, peeling off that paint, and bringing out, bit by the bit, the lovely wall paintings that those original monks had done, as a labor of love.

"Let us join the main party," suggested Mrs. Moreno, and they stepped out into the fragrant brightness of the garden, and went to where the group of students and the teacher stood, near the great empty reservoir tanks, underneath the balconies of the monastery.

There were many greetings, and the friendly hospitable group drew the little party into the gathering, and several people started to explain the tanks at once.

"They had to catch and preserve the rain water you see. . . ." "It is dry here, and they could not de-

pend entirely on wells or on rain either. They had
to get all the water they could, anyway, and store
it. . . ."

They wandered through the long corridors, where
due to the efforts of the men working to restore the
original frescoes, they could see quite well what the
convent must have looked like in the early days of
its founding. Lacing across the ceilings were bands
of design, crossed and crisscrossed in a rosy gray,
with little cherub faces looking out from between the
ribbons. Along the walls were paintings of scenes
from the Passion of Our Lord, and writings from the
Scriptures in Latin.

They went through the large beautiful place, along
the miradors, for there were lookouts, open to the
air, on all sides, each with a sweeping view of the
countryside, and through all the myriads of cells.

The dining hall and the great kitchens, and the
little pantry through which the foodstuffs were
passed into the dining hall, and the small altar from
which one of the monks read prayers and Scripture
while the others ate—they saw these last.

The teacher was talking.

"The paintings done on canvas, which are stored
here in a small dry room where they will not be
harmed, show you what quality of artists there were
among those men who came into this country, part of
a religious brotherhood, to spread their faith. There

must have been among them expert agriculturalists, engineers, architects, executives, artists. . . . In those days, I suppose, a man might join the church or enter a brotherhood, and then follow any one of a number of splendid careers, each with a great future in it, a great opportunity for advancement and service. . . ."

After a further trip about, and discussion of some of the paintings and frescoes from a technical point of view, he dismissed the classes to sketch as they would for an hour.

Judy was at her happiest now, watching a young woman get her paper out and start sketching, with pastels, the run-down garden.

"I like it here," confided Judy. "I would like to be a monk."

"You mean, a nun."

"Yes. I would like to be one, and live here and think high thoughts."

"We can think high thoughts anywhere."

"I suppose so."

"Just try for a little while," said the young woman, turning to the serious-eyed little girl and smiling at her. "Think high thoughts about the old old buildings here, the little garden, the flowers that they planted still blooming, the butterflies still hovering around, the same sun shining. . . ."

"There's nothing here that I could model," said

Judy after a while. "We are supposed to remember something to do in the art classes later, but how could I model a flower or a butterfly?"

"You'll find something to model if you search," said the girl, putting some more pink into the rose she was sketching. "I suggest that you look over there in those shadows, under those cool vines. . . ."

Judy went gingerly over, picking her steps, for in that part of the garden the shadows were deep and it looked ghostly.

She stepped quietly, she went in behind the long vines that dripped down off the wall.

Suddenly she gave a scream, and disappeared from sight.

The girl dropped her sketch pad and her pencils, spilled from her lap as she got up, rolled about the path. Two men and the art teacher ran after her toward where Judy had fallen.

The child had fallen into a sort of soft-earth pit behind the vines, and was scared but not much hurt. They pulled her out, dusted her off, and comforted her.

After a moment, when she had pulled her shoes and stockings off, to shake the dust out of them, Judy said, "There was something hard down there. Like stone or something."

"I wonder." The art teacher was hovering over the hole, looking down into it.

"I think I'll go bring one of the workmen," he said excitedly. "I think the little girl has found something. . . ."

He came in a few minutes, with the foreman in charge of the reconstruction crew, and two men who had been engaged in scraping off layers of paint to get down to the frescoes beneath in the dining hall.

"The little girl fell through a sort of cavey place here near the wall, and she says there's something hard down there, like stone, but I think it may be a find of some kind. . . . It looks like a hiding place,— as if these vines might have been trained down here this way to conceal it. . . ."

"We'll soon see."

Other people had gathered now, and there was a gabble of excited talk. Pollyanna put her arms around Judy.

"Are you all right darling?"

"Yes, I'm fine. It didn't hurt me. I may have discovered something, the man says."

Suddenly the shovels rang on stone. The dirt flew fast out of the hole, and after a moment there was a shout from the art teacher. "It's a trap door, of stone, with a heavy iron ring handle," he said. "We've got something! We owe it to you, little girl! We've found something!"

CHAPTER XVII

THE SECRET ROOM

"This may be awfully important," said the girl who had been sketching, to Judy. "Didn't I tell you?..."

It took them a long time to lift the stone door. Time had done its work in helping to cement it fast. They finally had to pry it loose, by running a strong pole of metal—something that the workmen had about—through the iron ring handle.

Little stone steps led downward into darkness.

"Now stand back, everyone," said the art teacher. "This may be dangerous. And even if it's not dangerous, this is not yet public property. We had better all go somewhere else, and interest ourselves in some sketching, and then return in an hour to get the opinion of the foreman. If he decides that we are not to go inside, we just aren't to go inside. Is that understood?"

There was a murmur of disappointed agreement. The art teacher's sleeve was plucked, timidly, and

190

he looked down to find Judy looking up at him imploringly.

"Couldn't I stay and watch?" she begged. "After all, I fell into the hole. If I hadn't. . . ."

The art teacher patted her cheek.

"You're a wheedler," he said. "But I guess we can let you stay."

He rapidly shepherded the others away though, and got them organized into sketching groups. This group doing the front elevation. This group doing the belfry tower as seen from the garden. This group doing an inside view of the kitchen and the great ovens.

He was an active man, dominating, a good teacher. He had put all his classes to work somewhere within twenty minutes, and then he came hurrying back to where Judy stood, interestedly looking down into the pit.

The foreman came carefully up the little stone steps, lighting his way with matches.

"I'll have to get a good light, candles or a lamp, before I can tell much about it," he said to the art teacher. "But it looks like quite a find. It looks like the treasure room. Secret. It is full of locked boxes, stored one on top of the other, and there is a little passage leading off to still another small room, where there are other boxes. I'll have to apply for permission to open them.

"Would you like to see the place, though?"

"Very much," answered Señor Torres, and immediately he felt a small moist hand slipped into his, and Judy said, "So would I."

"Wait until I get some candles," said the foreman, and he went away to where he had been working before Judy fell and there had been such a call for him.

"You're studying modeling, aren't you?" asked the teacher. "Not in my class. In Señor Ruiz's."

"Yes," said Judy.

"You're quite young to be interested in that." His gaze was curious. He had looked carefully into the small pointed face, with its wilful chin, sensitive mouth and nostrils, deep dreaming eyes.

"I like dancing the best," said Judy, "but Mother doesn't want me to start practicing here too soon. The altitude. I'm not used to it. And she thinks I'm delicate. I'm not, though. I'm strong. Feel my arm."

He felt her arm, seriously.

"You're growing fast; your mother is right not to let you overdo."

"I like modeling, though," said Judy, "because I love animals. I like to model them. I wouldn't care to model people."

"Why not?"

"I like people moving and thinking. Not just sitting, or posing."

"The good sculptor makes them move and think, even in stone."

"Really?"

"Yes. You must come into my class some day, and I'll arrange to show you some really fine statues, made by great sculptors, and you'll see what I mean."

"You're awfully nice," said Judy. "I'd love to."

The foreman came back with several small stubs of candle. He gave them to the art teacher to hold while he jumped down into the pit, and then he lighted them.

"Come along, if you like," he invited.

Señor Torres lowered Judy into the pit. The foreman caught her under the arms, and set her down gently. The art teacher himself then jumped down, and all three started down the little flight of steps, the foreman going ahead, Judy in the middle, and the art teacher following.

The candle threw flickering beams of light ahead of them, but it made the darkness even more gloomy. It was dampish, and there was a sickish smell, as of leather and musty silk.

"Here we are."

They had descended about fifteen steps, and they were steep. The candlelight revealed a room about

twelve feet square, and it was stacked h
side with chests and boxes.

"Oh, couldn't we open even one?" b
"I bet they're full of treasure."

The art teacher was staring at the box

"Well," the foreman was weakening
curiosity took hold of him too. "If w
open . . . we could look. I might have
thing about preserving them properly. .

The art teacher was examining every
to lift covers.

"Here is one," said Judy, "and it do
be really closed. . . ." She was point i
near the bottom of one of the piles.

"Let's see," and this time it was the f
self who spoke.

"Can you help me lift these others d
that we can see?"

"Of course."

Judy's tongue stuck to the top of her
throat felt dry. This was treasure.

But when they got the box open, a
edly turned back the cover of it, they
sheaves of papers, or parchment. Ro
and sheaves of it.

"Oh," said Judy, in a tremulous disap

She had hoped for the fire of rubies, the glow of pearls.

But the art teacher was examining some of the papers with interest, standing close to the candle.

"These are recipes," he said. "Probably secrets of the order. Wine recipes, liquors, medicines, bread, recipes for the sacred wafer. . . . Oh, this is wonderful! This is a treasure. . . ."

"Do you suppose all the boxes are full of just papers?" asked Judy.

"I don't know. But I doubt it."

The candles began to gutter. They had been only short stubs anyway.

"We must leave," said the foreman. "I shall cover this up again, and notify the authorities. If you will leave me your names and addresses, and where to reach you, I'll write and tell you as soon as I can if you can see all the things. Probably the little girl will receive a letter of thanks from the authorities, because we owe the discovery to her. . . ."

"Oh," cried Judy, flushing with pleasure. "When will I get the letter?"

"If they write one, and I think they will, it will come within the month," the foreman promised, as he lifted her out of the pit onto the garden path again.

Pollyanna stood there, waiting.

"Mother, it's wonderful," said Judy. "But I can't tell you about it, because we have to tell the authorities. It's a secret. But I'll get a letter thanking me for my discovery. And I'll bring you when I come to really see everything. Isn't it marvelous?"

"Yes," said Pollyanna, and her eyes met the amused but kind eyes of the foreman and the art teacher over the top of her little girl's head.

"Yes, it's marvelous," she said.

* * * * * * *

They were riding out from Actopan toward an Indian village near the foot of the mountains nearby. Señor Torres himself was riding with them, and explaining about the country. He had been over the road before, and knew it well.

"Do you see this road?" he asked. "Well, the Indians of this village made it themselves, so that they should have access to the main highway.

"And look. There are the telephone and electric light poles. The Indians themselves met in a sort of public council, after they had sold their first cooperative harvest from their land (the land was given to them after the Revolution under the land partition act) and decided to buy electric power for light from a power company. They themselves learned how to do the labor necessary in order to wire their village, and then they did it—all themselves."

Pollyanna looked out. The road was a fair graveled one, traveling straight as an arrow toward the foot of the hills, where a little village clung to the mountain slopes. Beside the road ran the poles and wires. And beyond in the fields, the corn was waving, and the alfalfa grew, and there were great burnished haystacks lying waiting for the fall, when the horses and burros would need the hay for feed.

"The Indians are naturally cooperative," explained Señor Torres, "and they share their work and their crops according to some system of their own which seems to work pretty well.

"There you see a pitiful little hut of the sort they used to live in before they were freed from peonage. What pleasure has a man in working the land, if his labor is not for himself, and the land is not his?"

"You are an idealist," said Pollyanna to him.

"Yes, I am," he answered fervently. "One must be. One must have courage and optimism. There is so much still to be done in the world."

They passed a place in the road where several Indian men were building a new house of stone.

"Let us stop and see it," impulsively exclaimed the young man. "The rest of the party will be waiting

for us at the school house in the village, but we
needn't stay here long."

The chauffeur stopped the car, and he and Judy,
Pollyanna, Anita, and Mrs. Moreno went over to
look at the little house.

The Indian workmen saw them coming and came
out to greet them. They took off their wide straw
hats, shook hands smilingly with everyone, and said,
"Buenos dias."

Then they showed the guests through their house
under construction, with quiet pride. It was going
to be a nice little house. The walls were thick and
strong, the floor was paved, and the rooms were well-
planned.

After everyone had walked through the little house
—there was still no roof on it—they shook hands
again, said farewells, and returned to the car.

"I wanted you to see," said the young art teacher,
"how well they build when they are encouraged to.
Those Indians had nothing to go by but a room plan.
They are natural architects. They build straight
and plumb and fine, but they don't know how they
do it.

"Have you seen the pyramids? You must. From
them you will gather whence the Indians get their
innate sense of symmetry and architecture."

"You are most enthusiastic," said Mrs. Moreno.

"If you wonder why, I will tell you," he said, "though I am not yet making it generally known. I am planning to leave the art school next year, and go into travel-teaching for the rural schools, teaching the Indians. I think there is a potential wealth of artists in Mexico that I would like to help discover."

"I think that's splendid," said Pollyanna.

"I have Indian blood in my veins," said the young man, "and I'm proud of it. I want to help those of them that are only now struggling upward."

The automobile stopped now in front of a simple but beautiful white building. The other automobiles had stopped, and the students and other teachers were out wandering about, pointing here and there to sights that interested them. One young man had already sat down on a rock, and was making a sketch of a little stone house, with its flower-garden, and its burro standing near, and an acacia tree dripping sweet yellow balls down on the grass.

Señor Torres called all the students together, and introduced the shy young Mexican of perhaps twenty-five who had emerged from the white building.

"Allow me to present Señor Rivas. He is the teacher here. And Mrs. Rivas, who also teaches."

A hatless young woman, in a simple cotton dress, her hair in shining black braids tied with red ribbon, came out and stood beside her husband.

"Mr. and Mrs. Rivas will show us through the school, and then will show us work done by the pupils. Please ask any questions you like. They will be happy to answer. Won't you?" And he turned to the young couple, who smiled quickly and immediately assented.

The school was a simple white room, with benches for the children to sit on. But it was clean and sunshiny and cheerful, and on the walls were lovely frescoes, telling the history of the little village, and showing the Indians at their labors in the fields, brown and peaceful among the golden sheaves of grain and corn.

"The people of the village built the school themselves," Mrs. Rivas explained. "Then they built these rooms as living quarters for us." She was showing them through a comfortable, scantily furnished, but beautiful set of rooms which the young people used as their home.

"Here," said Mrs. Rivas, "is some of the work done by the women of the village. They come to school whenever they can."

She proudly laid out some large white woolen bags, beautifully embroidered.

"They weave the cloth themselves," she said, "on hand looms, and then embroider it. Most of them make their own designs. See, here is where one of them has embroidered in her name—Maria. And here are some rugs. . . . They knew and remembered these crafts, and some of them made them to sell in the markets, but few of them made them for their own homes. Now they are all interested.

"The women have taken so well, too, to my little talks on cookery and on home hygiene. A doctor comes once a year to vaccinate against smallpox. At first, they were afraid of it, and resisted. But just the other day, one woman brought her new-born baby to me, and asked how far it was to the nearest doctor with the medicine. She meant to walk all the way, to make sure that her baby would be safe."

Pollyanna looked at her closely. She was probably part Indian, but her manners were city manners and her lovely face and hair looked as if they had not been exposed too often to the hot sun. Mrs. Rivas looked up quickly and caught the look. She smiled and answered it.

"I am from Mexico City," she said. "I dress this way so that the women here will not be envious, or think me 'putting on airs.' Besides, I like it now. I like going hatless in the sun, feeling my cheeks glow, feeling my arms getting brown like the good soil."

"I believe," said Pollyanna, "that all you teachers are poets in Mexico."

"Now let us go back into the schoolroom," said Mrs. Rivas, "and I will show you some of the work the children do."

She brought out pages of writing, neat and careful. There were arithmetic papers. And little drawings. Some of the drawings were remarkably vivid, sturdy, and original. "How good these are," murmured Pollyanna.

"They are gifted," said Mrs. Rivas. "Their natural gift is painting. And architecture. But they love music too. Look. Here is the piano the people bought last year after harvest."

It was a simple player piano, but electrically wired.

"They have many records, and they love to play them," said Mrs. Rivas. "At night, when work is done, and on Sundays, they come here, and play and listen, and dance.

"The harvests were good. After each man was paid a good share, there was money left over. With that the people bought the piano, and a truck. They carry their harvests to market in the truck, and on Sundays the children get rides. It is cooperatively owned. Next they will buy a radio."

"It must be thrilling to watch such happiness, such development," said Pollyanna.

"It thrills me," said Mrs. Rivas, simply. "Let us

join the others now. They are going over to the
theatre."

"Oh, is there a theatre?"

"Yes, indeed."

Several little children had come into the schoolroom, shy but curious, their big straw hats in their
hands. Mrs. Rivas greeted them all. But as she
started to leave one of them pulled her sleeve, and
whispered a request.

"Of course," she answered. "But be careful. Roll
the record back carefully, the way I showed you."

"Oh I will," came the eager whispered assurance.

And as they left, Pollyanna saw the little boy
scamper to the piano with shining eyes. She lingered
to watch him deftly adjust the record, switch on the
current, and start pedaling. The music flowed out
of the piano, steadily. His little body swayed rhyth-
mically on the piano seat.

As Pollyanna followed Mrs. Rivas toward another building she saw many little children running
toward the schoolhouse. They heard the music.
They were drawn as with magnets.

Mrs. Rivas saw them too, and spoke to Pollyanna.

"I can see that you are very sympathetic to our
work."

"Yes," cried Pollyanna. "Isn't every one?"

"But of course not. This has all come since the lands were divided, and of course many people still feel very badly about that. Others think that the Indians are not worth all this effort to educate them. Still others feel that in the end it will only make the Indians unhappy, discontented with what they have, yet unable to get more."

"I can see that there are many groups of opinion here, as everywhere," said Pollyanna. "But I like seeing people happy. And who knows what the future will bring for any of us. We may as well do what seems right and kind at the moment."

"I feel like that," said Mrs. Rivas, and throughout the rest of their stay she was close to Pollyanna, answering her questions, and supplying her with much information in passing.

They saw the community building, where meetings of all the citizens were held. They saw the open-air theatre, where plays, speeches, and movies were given, whenever a traveling group from the Central Department in Mexico City arrived, and where pupils under Mrs. Rivas's direction sometimes gave little plays of their own. They visited the hospital, and some of the homes, where they were received with the utmost cordiality, and with a certain quiet charm that princes could envy in its poise and gentleness.

Then there were adieus, and the little sketching groups that had fallen by the wayside were gathered up and marshalled into automobiles again, and the day was over. The cavalcade was en route to Mexico City once more.

"Did you like it?" asked Mrs. Moreno. "It has been almost too much for my silent little Anita? Eh, baby? Are you tired?" Anita was leaning against her mother's arm, sleepy-eyed.

"I'm not very sleepy," protested the little girl. "I'm hungry, though."

"Hungry! Do you know what we've done, Mrs. Pendleton? We've forgotten the picnic. As soon as we come to a nice place we'll stop and eat it."

The chauffeur from the front seat spoke.

"I was wondering when you'd think of the lunch," he said.

"It is a tribute to the expedition that we all forgot," said Pollyanna.

CHAPTER XVIII

LANDSLIDES AND CLUES

JIMMY, Junior and Aguilar sat about their camp-fire drinking hot chocolate and finding even the warmth of the cups they held grateful, for the mountain nights were cold and a wind had come up that chilled them to the marrow.

They had been in camp a week. A few workmen crouched over their own fire, and got ready to huddle into their blankets in their tents. Jimmy was not ordering any more men until he had found the opening he sought.

"Well," said Junior, "it just seems as if we ought to get somewhere soon."

"I'm glad it's summer and a rather dull season for me, or I don't know what would become of my law practice," said Aguilar. "I've got some friends handling it for me for a while, but after a while clients get tired of being shunted off."

"We can only keep trying," said Jimmy. "I've got to show some results here pretty soon too, or my reputation as an engineer is not so good."

206

They sipped their chocolate in silence. Suddenly there was a roar, and a rushing sound, and a ripping and tearing.

"What's that?"

"Sounds like a landslide," said Jimmy. "Rather a big one."

Rumblings sounded for some time, and then the last bumps as a big boulder followed the others down and finally came to rest.

"We can look it up in the morning," said Jimmy, easily. "It must have been on the other side of the mountain."

But scarcely had he finished saying the words when another roaring and ripping, sounding much closer to them, rent the air, and the valley floor seemed to tremble with the shock of the fall of the rock and earth

"Whew!" Jimmy whistled. "Getting closer to us."

And there came another roar and shaking, and then, unmistakably, where they sat, the ground heaved and rolled, as if it were a sea.

"Earthquake!"

The workmen had come out, and were trembling and silent near Jimmy.

"Keep calm, fellows. There's nothing we can do. Don't lose your heads."

Junior took his father's arm. He was pale, but silent.

It was over in a moment. There had been no damage.

"Very slight shake," said Jimmy. "Enough to start rocks rolling and land falling off the hill, but not a bad quake really. We're lucky."

"What shall we do, Dad?" asked Junior in a small but steady voice. "Shall we go to bed, or wait for the next one?"

"We'd better go to bed," said Jimmy decisively speaking to the men, who were still standing about, rather apprehensive. And to set an example, he shook hands with Aguilar, and piloted Junior ahead of him.

"Come on, boy," he said. "We'll turn in, too."

An hour later the whole camp was silent.

Junior had been badly frightened. He hadn't shown it, but now he felt the reaction. He couldn't sleep. He moved so that he could see out of the tent a little. He looked up at the black sky, where millions of stars seemed to be gently revolving, miles high, and shining like diamonds.

Something of their distance, their cold glowing that had been for centuries and would be for many more, comforted him, as it has comforted many others. "I guess I just don't matter so much," he

thought, vaguely, and somehow that feeling assuaged
his fears. He slept.

*   *   *   *   *   *   *

The morning was bright, satiny-blue and soft, like
new ribbon. The workmen were up and at their
breakfast, laughing and gay as people are likely to
be after they have been worried, when the danger is
gone.

"Eat plenty, everyone," called Jimmy gaily, after
his wash in the icy lake-water. "I have a hunch
there's going to be plenty of work today.

"Aguilar, you take half the men and start exploring the far half of the mountain. I'll take the rest
and go the other side. Those landslides may indicate something to us."

"Who shall I go with, Dad?" asked Junior, sling-
ing his camera over his shoulder.

"Come along with me," said Jimmy.

After breakfast they started out. They could
faintly see, about half-way up the mountain, a
jagged place, grayish red in color, where the slide
had started.

"We'll make for that first," ordered Jimmy.

He and Junior started. The men of his party,
shouldering shovels, followed along after them.

It was a longer climb than it looked.   It was fully
two hours later, and the shirts on the backs of all the
men were wet in patches from perspiration, when
they came upon the main place left bare by the slide.
And Jimmy gave a jubilant shout, for now, showing
obviously dark against the gray soil, was an opening
into the mountain.

"Boys, we've got our mine!" he called.   "Get in
there, and start clearing that tunnel!   Hey wait.
Before you start.   How about a picture of it, Junior?
Is the light right?"

"I can make it right, Dad."

Junior busied himself adjusting something over
the lense of his camera, and sighting it carefully.
He took a couple of views of the little opening there
in the hillside, an opening that held promise, mystery, death. . . .

"Okay, Dad."

"Now, men."

They had been working some time, enlarging the
entrance. Then, little by little, Jimmy ventured inside.   After a little while he came out again.

"Are you tired, Junior?"

"No."

"How about going to find Aguilar, and telling
him what we've got here.   He may have found something himself.   If he has, just tell him about this,

and let him alone. If he hasn't, he might like to come over here. Then you had better go on back down to camp and wait for us. I don't want you getting worn out. You could take a long-distance view of the tunnel opening from the valley floor, if you can get it into focus."

"Okay, Dad."

Junior looked about him, and decided to take the ridge down a certain distance, and then cross over two more until he could get within hailing distance of Aguilar. It would take some time. Yes, Dad was right. It would be mid-afternoon before he could get to Aguilar.

He toiled along the ridges, through the rough brush, picking his way carefully. It was indeed about mid-afternoon when he came in sight of Aguilar and his party. They had been busy excavating around the other landslide.

Junior began to call and wave his arms when he thought he was within hailing distance. But the light breeze evidently carried his voice away, or else they were making so much noise with their shovels and picks that they did not hear him. Nobody noticed him, or paid any attention, as a matter of fact, until they were almost on him. And when Junior got near, he saw what they had found. A human skull. . . .

"Mr. Aguilar."

"Eh? Oh, Junior. Hello!"

"Is that a skull?"

"No. Look." Aguilar picked it up. His hands were trembling with excitement.

"It is stone."

"Gee whiz. Was it petrified?"

"I don't think so. I think it was carved. We can learn that for certain later. And we have come upon stone, hard, square, chiseled stone. . . ."

"Well," said Junior, "Dad has found a tunnel, and he's been in it. He says to tell you he's got his mine, if you want to come over. But I guess you don't want to leave."

"Not just now. It looks as if we had come upon a sort of wall . . . but here, buried in the mountain. . . ."

"Didn't they cover up a lot of their buildings, the Indians, for fear the Spanish would find them and tear them down?"

"Yes, they did, but this is a real mountain Junior. Not just earth thrown up to cover a pyramid."

"How do you know? Father Mestres was telling me the Indians did lots of things people can't explain, things that seemed impossible."

"Well, we've found something, anyway. I think I'll stay here until sundown, though. We can all talk over our finds at supper tonight."

"I guess you're glad you came in with my Dad," said Junior. "Aren't you?"

"It was for me, a lucky break, as you say."

"Wouldn't you like me to take a picture of that stone skull, just where you found it?"

"That's a grand idea."

"I think I could take a clear one of a little of that wall, where it shows, too," said the boy, squinting at his lens.

"Great."

Junior stood and watched proceedings for a while. Inch by inch, very carefully, for Aguilar did not want to mar any carving or the surface of the smooth stones, they were uncovering what was undoubtedly a man-made structure of some kind. The stones were dark-gray, almost black, with pink markings.

Junior began to descend slowly into the valley.

Suddenly he stopped. "But there were three slides," he thought to himself, "and Dad and Señor Aguilar have each found and started work in one. Maybe I can find another. . . ."

But he was very tired, and he knew his father would not want him to risk being caught on the mountain after dark. So he continued downward, zigzagging along a steep ridge.

Alive now to the discoveries, the excitement and the adventure of what was happening, he cast curious eyes on every stone in his path, and even kicked some of them over and examined them with his hands. He would have liked very much indeed, to find something himself.

But though his journey down to camp should have taken him two hours, and it took him three and a half, he found nothing.

"Not even an arrow head," he muttered to himself unhappily. "Well, anyway, I've got the pictures."

CHAPTER XIX

A PACT

RUTH sat in the patio, unhappy. She was lonesome. Nancy was gone, and wouldn't ever come back any more, Mother had said. Nancy was dead. But now Daddy and Junior had been gone such a long time too. Could they be. . . . No. It couldn't be.

Mother had taken Judy to the art class again, and Judy made so many little mud and clay models of things now that she didn't want to play with Ruth. And there were no other little girls, only Anita. And Anita lived all the way across town. Ruth only saw Anita once or twice a week.

It was really awfully long since Daddy and Junior. . . . And no letters had come. She felt miserable in her stomach. Empty.

The emptiness increased and began to gnaw. Ruth rose and went into the kitchen, thinking she would ask for a biscuit, or a banana, or something. But Lolita wasn't in the kitchen that moment. Ruth tried the back door, that let out on a tiny alley, and found it open. She just couldn't help going out.

She went across the street, and into the cathedral gardens. There was nobody there, but it was nice. There were flower bushes taller than she was, under which she could walk, looking up at the sky through the green leaves as if she were under special little trees. She liked that.

There was also a cat that she had seen sometimes, a big black cat with white whiskers, that hunted for gophers in the garden. Perhaps she could find it. She began to look, methodically and quietly.

But she couldn't find the cat, and her disappointment, and her vague feeling that something was wrong somewhere, came over her again. She sat down under a rosebush and gave herself up to tears.

"Ruthie, why do you cry?"

It was Jose, the bell ringer's boy. He had been out marketing. His arms were full of small bundles. He wiped Ruth's eyes and fat wet cheeks with his hand, because he didn't have a handkerchief. It was the comforting touch, the companionship, that Ruth needed.

"I'm crying because Junior and Daddy are dead too. Like Nancy. Nancy went away and didn't come back and didn't come back, and then Mama told me she was dead. And now Daddy and Junior don't come back. . . ."

Jose had started at first. But now he smiled understandingly. He sat down under the rosebush, and put his arm around Ruth.

"But they will come back, I know," he said.

Ruth sniffed still. She was so happy at having a friend for a while that she did not immediately relinquish the tears. A woman's trick; she learned it early.

"Did you get a letter?" she asked. "We didn't. Mama said they were where they couldn't write letters. But she said that about . . . about. . . ." The whole picture rose vividly in her mind again. She had convinced herself. She wept again, aloud, and bitterly.

Jose began to unwrap one of his packages. He took from it a piece of sweet sticky candy, and silently gave Ruth a piece. She stopped crying, though her small bosom still rose spasmodically, and her last tears crept slowly down her cheeks and spilled off her round chin. She tasted the candy.

Jose ate a piece too.

"Isn't that good?" he asked.

"Yes."

"I'll tell you something. I would like to have a girl. A favorite girl. Will you be mine?"

"But if I do, Judy will be mad."

"Judy?"

"She's so stuck on you, she looks over here where you live all the time."

Jose said nothing. He quickly ate another piece of candy, and chewed hard. So did Ruth.

"I could be your second-best girl," ventured Ruth timidly.

"All right. I'll be your second-best beau."

"But who'll be my first?"

"Anybody you like better than me."

"But I like you the best."

"Well, if you want to, you can always pick out somebody else for your best beau."

"Well, all right," agreed Ruth, after thought.

"Does your mother know you're here?"

"No." Ruth whispered the word.

"Well, I'd better take you home, then, or she'll be worrying."

"All right."

Ruth rose obediently, and straightened her short yellow dress.

* * * * * * *

At supper that evening, over her chocolate and buttered buns, with a brown ring of the sweet liquid showing around her mouth, Ruth said, "Mama, why don't we get letters from Daddy and Junior?"

Pollyanna answered.

"Why, baby, I told you that they were far up in the mountains, where no postman goes or comes."

Ruth put down her cup, and her lip trembled. The same sad thought had intruded again.

"But that's . . . that's what you said about Nancy. . . ."

"Darling." Pollyanna got up from her seat at the table, and went round to where Ruth sat, round and disconsolate.

"You must believe Mama. Nothing has happened to Daddy and Junior. They'll be home again soon. I never told you that dear Nancy was coming home again, did I?"

"No."

"So, you must believe me. Do you?"

"Yes."

Judy was silent. But when the bells began sounding their last song of the day, her face brightened, and a radiant, yet a secret look glowed in her eyes.

"After supper Judy will show you what she made today," Pollyanna told Ruth.

"What did you make, Judy?"

"Well, it's nothing really. It's just a little model of a bell."

"Is it for me?"

Judy flushed, and hesitated.

"I know," said Ruth, "it's for Jose."

Judy paled and got a little defiant.

"What if it is?"

"I bet he'll like it," said Ruth. "I was talking to him today, over in the garden by the church."

"What did he say?" asked Judy eagerly. A sort of shyness had come over her since Junior had been away. She never went to the garden, or to see Jose. She saw him only on the days when Father Mestres had the children over to study Spanish.

"He said he wanted me to be his girl," said Ruth, honestly.

Judy's eyes widened, and her mouth fell open unhappily.

"I said, No, I couldn't be his first girl, because you were so stuck on him, but I could be his second-best." Ruth was eating more biscuit now, happy to have the center of the stage and to be leading the conversation.

Judy rose suddenly and left the table without a word. Ruth watched her go with puzzled eyes.

"What's the matter with her, Mama?"

Pollyanna sighed.

"She's growing up, Ruthie. It's painful."

"Does it really hurt, Mama?"

"It hurts awfully."

"But we have to grow up, don't we Mama?"

"Yes we do."

* * * * * * *

Mrs. Moreno and Anita came to see Pollyanna and her two little girls that afternoon. They were excited, shining-eyed, fluttery.

"We're going on a trip with Papa!" said Anita. "Papa is going to take us over his big road, all the way to San Antonio!"

Mrs. Moreno and Pollyanna began talking about plans, wardrobes, and luggage.

"Do you know, I have never been to the United States," said Mrs. Moreno, "except to New York, once, and I was only there long enough to take a steamer to France. Ramon is going to drive us, with him, over his road, and then we are going on up through the United States to New York. We'll be away about three months. I hope you will not be gone when we get back."

"It's hard to say," said Pollyanna. "I go wherever my husband's work takes him, if I possibly can. We are too often separated as it is. But I do hope I can be here to welcome you back again, and to hear how you liked your first visit to the States."

"I shall buy clothes! Ramon gave me a present of money to spend, just for American clothes, in New York," exulted Mrs. Moreno. "It will be like another honeymoon—except for Anita."

"I'm coming on your honeymoon," said Anita.

"I would like to give you some letters to friends of mine," said Pollyanna, "though I don't doubt that you will make so many new friends that it will be hard to remember all their names, or find time for them."

"I am so excited," said Mrs. Moreno. "Did I tell you the reason we are going? My husband is going to give some lectures on the road, before a convention of engineers, and will also talk to students in two or three universities, in the engineering courses. It is a great honor. He is very proud, and so am I."

"He deserves those honors," said Pollyanna. "And you deserve the good times you are going to have. When are you leaving?"

"We are leaving next week, on Thursday."

"Will you let me give you a little farewell dinner, here, just our families,—and perhaps Señor Bello from the Conservatory, who went with us that day to the mountains, when we heard the little fiesta. Let us say on Tuesday evening. I believe Jimmy and Junior will be back for the week-end, and perhaps Señor Aguilar. Let us say, Monday. I know I could persuade them to stay over one day. Would that be a good day for you?"

"Splendid, I think. I'll ask Ramon, and then I'll let you know. Ramon will want to see Mr. Pendleton again before he goes. He will be very disappointed if he does not."

"Well, we will say Monday then. And I will cook an American dinner—a typical American dinner—to get you used to the food you will eat in the States!"

"With chocolate cake, Mama?"

"Yes!"

"And hot cakes?" asked Mrs. Moreno. "Ramon loves hot cakes. He eats them all the time in the United States."

"And hot cakes," promised Pollyanna, laughing, "even if it is dinner!"

CHAPTER XX

Judy had brought the bell back to the art class. It seemed very imperfect to her. Silly. She looked at it disconsc'.tely, and fumbled with her mass of greenish-clay. She didn't like any of the models that stood about on the balcony. She didn't feel like doing anything, and yet she was restless. It was early in the afternoon, and the sun shone down through the central court, open to the sky, of the big building. The warm sun burned through the thin voile of Judy's dress, comfortably. It made her feel sleepy. She sat there, her idle fingers in the clay, dreaming.

But at a touch on her shoulder, she started. It was Señor Torres, the art teacher who had gone with them to Actopan.

"We're famous," he said to her, smiling.

Judy looked bewildered.

"Do you remember that pit where you fell down through, behind the vines in the convent courtyard?

224

Remember the secret room down under the ground, where we saw all the chests?"

"Oh yes!" Judy clasped her hands. Excitement! Life was assuming proper proportions again.

"Well, experts have gone through every chest, and they say it is a great treasure of documents. The National Library of Mexico says they are immensely valuable! There is a photographer here who wants to take your picture and talk to you a minute."

"To me?"

"Yes. You are the discoverer, really. He just wants you to tell him about it."

"Oh." Judy began to tremble a bit, and her mouth felt dry.

"I'll go with you," said the art teacher. "He's waiting down in the court."

Judy wiped off her clayey fingers, and smoothed her hair. She pulled down her dress.

"Do I look all right?" she whispered.

"You look very pretty."

They went down the broad long stairways, and into the court. There were some pupils sketching there in the court, but a young man, camera in hand, had cleared a little space against a sunny piece of wall, and there he guided Judy and Señor Torres.

"First we'll get your pictures, one of you together and then one of each of you alone, and then we'll have a little talk. We can go into one of the rooms for that. I've arranged to get one free."

The other students, in the smocks, seated on folding chairs, picked up their chairs, and moved away, so as to allow room for a good picture. They all watched. They looked at Judy smilingly, and she felt happy to be noticed. Most of them were so much older than she. Some of them had never even known she was alive until that moment. She felt herself expanding happily to be the center of all attention.

She and the art teacher, who refused to take off his smock or his horn-rimmed glasses, stood against the wall, and the warm stones felt good against Judy's back. Then there was a picture of Judy alone. The art teacher wouldn't let them take his picture alone.

"I had nothing to do with it," he said impatiently. "I was only among those present. It was due to the little girl, to Miss Pendleton, that the things were found."

Judy found herself being propelled gently toward one of the rooms where the reporter confused her by taking out a pencil and a few pieces of folded paper and asking her some questions.

"What is your name?"

"Judy Pendleton."

"What is your father's name?"

"James Pendleton."

"What does he do?"

"He's an engineer."

"Is he working in Mexico, or do you live here all the time?"

"He's just here for a little while."

After getting her age, her address, and the names of her sister and brother, the reporter suddenly stopped asking her questions, and looked up at her with a bright, eager gaze.

"I'm sorry to have to bother you with these questions, but you know, we are expected to get certain information." He smiled, and Judy smiled back at him quickly.

"Now, if you'll just tell me about how you happened to find the pit and the secret rooms at the convent. . . ."

Judy thought a minute. Her imagination was vivid and accurate. She put herself back in the convent garden that sunny afternoon. She was talking to the girl who was sketching. It all came back, every moment of it.

"I went to look for something, and I remember thinking there might be some little toads or something, or maybe a little cat, over there behind those

thick vines.   There seemd to be a space behind them.
I went in back of them, and. . . ."

* * * * * * *

Going back upstairs to her class afterward, Judy
felt glowing.

"They're going to let us see the things, aren't
they?" she asked Señor Torres.

"Yes. We can see them at the Library. All the
manuscripts are being taken to the library, and they'll
be kept there. The chests will go to the museum,
though of course they will keep some of them at the
convent itself, for people to see.

"I'll come and get you and your mother and take
you to the library, as soon as they let me know when
they will be available for us to see. You won't understand them, and neither will I, but it will be something to remember, won't it?"

"Oh yes!" breathed Judy.

And almost as soon as she had sat down to her
modeling again, she decided to make an image,—a
small one—of one of those chests. She was happily
molding it and carving in little designs with her
finger-nail, when Pollyanna arrived to take her home.

Pollyanna was dressed in a white woolen suit,
with white gloves, shoes, and tight little hat, under-

neath which her charmingly kind and sweet face, and her smooth yellow hair, glowed in the sunshine.

Many of the students lifted their eyes from their work and smiled at her as she ascended the stairs to the broad balcony where Judy was, for she had come every day that Judy was in class, and her quiet natural charm was soon felt and watched for.

"Mother, look, I've made a little model of what those chests underneath the convent garden at Acto-pan looked like. One of them had little designs of lilies sort of cut into the leather, like this. . . ."

"That's very nice," said Pollyanna. "I like it. And I like the bell that you made the other day, too. What have you done with that?"

"It's here."

"I think," said Pollyanna, "that it would be nice to give that little bell to Jose. I want to drop in to see how his father is, and to ask Jose something. You could come along with me, if you like. I thought I would go there before we go home.

"But meanwhile, I want to go shopping to buy some things for our dinner party on Tuesday."

"Oh Mother, I love to go shopping!"

Judy went to her locker and put away her clay, cleaned her hands carefully, and put on her hat.

"Mother," she said, as they walked along the street toward the central shopping district, "a reporter come today to talk to me and take my picture. He was asking all about the secret place under the garden at the convent in Actopan. I don't know when my picture will be in the paper. Maybe to-morrow."

"What paper?"

"El Excelsior."

"We'll buy it tomorrow and see. Judy, how ex-citing! You are getting to be a celebrity. Pretty soon you'll be charging us to let us live in the same house with you."

"Ah, Mama!"

"I shall have to move out, if my children are going to be famous. I shall feel too humble and undis-tinguished."

"Mama!"

Judy began to laugh. She felt suddenly happy. She was going to be in the paper,—and she was going to see Jose. What a good day!

Pollyanna ordered roasting chickens from the market, to be delivered Monday, and honey, and vegetables, and the makings of a real old-fashioned chocolate cake.

"Now comes the surprise," said Pollyanna. "I am going to buy you and Ruth new dresses for the party."

"Oh Mother, how lovely!"

The big store was cool, and some of the fragrance from the perfume counter lingered around the section of the store where the children's dresses were on sale.

For Judy they selected a blue dress, with a trimming of white organdy. The ruffled organdy collar rose around her small face like the petals of a flower.

For Ruth Pollyanna chose a pink dress, with a design of little fat white rabbits prancing around the hem.

"But aren't you going to buy yourself a new dress, Mama?"

"No darling."

"What one will you wear?"

"My blue lace dress."

"Well, you look wonderful in that," said Judy.

Pollyanna suddenly realized what was happening. She was beginning to discuss clothes with her daughter.

"Dear me, dear me," she thought, half ruefully, "she is growing up, really. It won't be long before my daughters will be gently but firmly making me over, as I did Aunt Ruth."

And she had to laugh out loud at that thought, remembering the far-off days of her childhood, after she had gone to live with Aunt Ruth in Vermont. Aunt Ruth had been so severe, so prim, so tight of

hair and lip and mind.   But little by little Pollyanna
had softened them—and the result had been that
Aunt Ruth had blossomed into a delayed happiness.

"Perhaps it's as well that young people do take
us over, like problems to be solved," she thought.

They finished their shopping, and took a taxi. As
they rolled along through the streets, and out of
busy Mexico City into their quiet, still, fragrant suburb, Judy sat very still, and was quiet.

"I am going to ask Jose to play the bells himself
that evening, while we are all at dinner," said Pollyanna.   "Señor Bello will be with us, and I want him
to hear Jose.   I think the boy is talented, and of
course he is very poor.   Perhaps, if Señor Bello
thinks he has real talent, he may arrange for Jose to
have a scholarship, and study music at the Conservatory."

Judy's face glowed with pleasure.

"Oh, I'm sure he'll want to do that for Jose when
he hears him; don't you think so, Mother?"

"I'm not sure, darling.   I don't know a thing
about music.   I think Jose is talented.   But I may
be wrong.   We must not get up too much hope.
And we must not tell Jose why we are asking him
to play the bells that evening.   Because if Señor
Bello doesn't say anything, I shouldn't want Jose to

feel badly and be disappointed. So don't mention it, ever, will you?"

"No Mama."

When the taxi stopped with them in front of the cathedral, Pollyanna and Judy saw that they would not have to ascend the long steep stairs into the balcony to find Jose, or to inquire about his father.

Jose and Ruth were sitting with Father Mestres, at the little rough garden table, with pencils and paper before them.

Pollyanna and Judy walked up the path, smelling the sweet scent of sun-warmed blossoms, and hearing the twittering of birds and the buzzing of crickets and bees. The black cat with the white whiskers was hunting, with twitching tail, but paused a moment, as they walked past, to greet them, and then returned to whatever prey it was stalking.

"Good afternoon, Mrs. Pendleton," said Father Mestres. "I had an hour to myself this afternoon, so I have been reading some history to Ruth and Jose. How do you do, Judy."

"Good afternoon, Father. May we listen?"

"I think we must call this the end of the lesson," said Father Mestres.

Judy startled herself and her mother by her words

"Father Mestres," said she, "here is a little model

of a bell that I made in my class. Would you like it?"

"I am delighted to have it," Father Mestres replied seriously. "Thank you very much. I will keep it in my study."

Jose rose to excuse himself, but Pollyanna detained him a moment.

"Is your father quite well again, Jose?"

"Yes, thank you. He does not play the bells so often, because he must not get too tired, but then I am happy to have the practice."

"You love the bells, don't you?"

"Yes, I do."

"And you love music?"

"Oh, yes." He seemed a little surprised by her questions. He could not imagine anyone not loving music and the bells. He had been brought up with them, he had heard their voices more often than the voices of men.

"I wanted to ask you a favor, Jose. I am having some special guests to dinner on Tuesday night. And I want them to be sure to hear the bells. Will you play them, yourself—something specially beautiful —if Father Mestres will permit?"

His face lighted happily at the request, and he turned impulsively to Father Mestres.

"I am delighted that my carilloneur is so honored," said Father Mestres, smiling.

"I'll go to tell Father," said Jose, and he went swiftly through the garden.

Pollyanna turned to where Judy sat, following the boy with her eyes.

"Judy, take Ruthie home with you now and show her the present we bought her."

"Oh, have I got a present?" Ruth stood up, dropping a lapful of flowers she had picked in the patio at home.

"I shall stay a moment," said Pollyanna. "I want to chat with Father Mestres. Can you spare me a moment now, Father?"

"I am delighted," said he.

The two little girls crossed the garden and then the street. Both Pollyanna and Father Mestres watched until they were safe on the other side. Then Father Mestres turned to Pollyanna, quietly and expectantly.

"I don't know whether I was presuming in asking that the bells be played specially for us on Tuesday," she said. "But I will tell you why I suggested it. I have invited Señor Bello, the head of the National Conservatory of Music for that evening, and I am hoping that I may persuade him to arrange some sort

of musical scholarship for the boy.   Somehow I felt
that if I could, it might be pleasing to you, too—in
a small way a return to you for all your kindness to
my children.   I know that you are very fond of
Jose."

"Indeed I am.   And I think he is very talented.   I
am happy that you have thought of this.   God bless
you."

"Thank you, Father."

Pollyanna rose to go.   They shook hands.

"Vaya Ud. con Dios," said Father Mestres, as
she started down the path of the sunshiny garden
toward the street.

CHAPTER XXI

WHAT THEY SAW IN THE MOUNTAIN

"Oh Jimmy, I'm so glad you're home!"

Jimmy had a growth of beard, and Junior was tanned and brown as a berry. Señor Aguilar was unshaven too, and they were all dirty, tired, excited, and hungry. It was Sunday morning. Aguilar's automobile stood outside, loaded with gear, and the three had come bursting into the little pink house to find Pollyanna and the two girls at late breakfast in the sunshiny patio.

"Mr. Aguilar may wash and shave first," cried Pollyanna. "Then Jimmy. Then Junior. Meanwhile, here's coffee for all of you. And I'll make some biscuits while you're getting cleaned up for a large breakfast. Then I want to hear everything. All about everything!"

Then the house hummed. Everyone was shouting and laughing. When it was Jimmy's turn, he sang in the tub, and out of the corner of his mouth while he was shaving,—very much off tune. Junior talked constantly in a high excited voice, and was in a fever

237

of disappointment that shops were closed so that he could not buy some developing material that he needed. Mr. Aguilar said he had completely forgotten his practice, and the law, and his bills, and letters, and probably he was ruined. Lolita confided to Pollyanna that she had better stay to cook dinner—though Sunday evening was usually hers to do with as she wished, because she said she felt sure that the señora would have enough to do, just listening.

About an hour later the table was rearranged, and freshly laden with hot food, coffee, and fruit.

"Um! This tastes wonderful. We haven't had anything like this for days. Our food ran a little short there at the end."

"About one meal a day!" Junior exclaimed, bitter with the memory of it.

"Say, that isn't so," said Jimmy. "Coffee and bread for breakfast, chocolate for lunch, and beans for supper. What more do you want?"

"Jimmy? Why didn't you get more supplies?" Pollyanna dreaded the thought of her boy going hungry.

Jimmy was piling his plate with freshly scrambled eggs and helping Mr. Aguilar to his "seconds." Junior was having more bacon and lathering a biscuit thoroughly with butter and honey.

"Didn't hurt him. Got to get used to that sort of

thing if he's going to rough it anywhere.   The point is, darling, we've made discoveries.   Such exciting discoveries that it was more fun to dig than eat, and that's the truth."

"How could it be?" asked fat Ruth looking up from her bananas and cream.

"Well," answered Jimmy, with dancing eyes, "long long ago there were people living here in Mexico called. . . ."

"Aztecs," Ruth interrupted, taking another bite. "Where did you hear that?"

"Father Mestres read it to me out of a book."

"Well, did he tell you that even before the Aztecs there were others, and before them, others, and so on, way, way back into history?"

"No, he didn't," Ruth replied.   "But there's more to the book that he hasn't read to us.   Maybe he will tell us about them."

"Well," said Jimmy, making an impressive silence, and looking straight into his wife's eyes, "we have found things—gold and jewelry and weapons and dishes used by Indians who lived here in Mexico many many thousands of years before the Aztecs."

"Where?"   This from Judy.

"In Miss Aguamonte's mine"

"Oh Jimmy!" Pollyanna's voice was mixed dismay and incredulity and joy.

"Why sound sad about it?"

"But if you found historical treasures, what about poor Miss Aguamonte, who needs the money. . . . She doesn't own these treasures, does she?"

"No, they won't be hers. But I am sure some sort of handsome settlement will be made for her. She can prove positively that the mine itself is hers. Furthermore, it's my opinion that it can be worked for ore, later, after the jewels and dishes and what not are removed."

"And jewels and gold are not all of what we've found!"

"What else?"

"A sort of altar inside the mountain—an extraordinary thing. A concealed pyramid. It looks as though it had been a kind of altar of death, for there are graves inside the mountain—where we found the jewels there are human bones. . . . And the small pyramid and the walls that surround it have death's heads carved on them. . . ."

"Oh Jimmy, it seems unbelievable." Pollyanna looked down at her own pink hands on the white tablecloth, at her children and her husband placidly eating.

"It can't be true!" she exclaimed.

"It is, though. I can prove it. I brought you some of the things, to show you."

"What?"

"They aren't presents, honey. We have to leave everything exactly as we found it, of course, and arrange with the government and with the museum to have them visit the mountain as soon as possible, and collect and care for the treasures, and decide what is to be done about the pyramid."

"Then you won't be going back for a while?"

"Not for several days. For perhaps a week. By the way," Jimmy cautioned his little family, "you children are to say absolutely nothing about this to anyone. Not to a living soul."

Ruth dropped her spoon.

"Because," went on Jimmy, "we didn't have very many men that we could get to stay there on guard, and no thieves must get near the place, or we are ruined, and it would be terrible!"

"I've taken some peachy pictures, Mother," said Junior, "but I couldn't get half enough. I had plenty of film with me, but not as many magnesium bulbs as I wanted. I could only get a few pictures of the pyramid-altar inside the mountain. Mother, it's wonderful! I wish you could see it! I hope the pictures turn out well; they'll give you some idea."

"Well," Pollyanna turned to Mr. Aguilar, "I have an idea that you will abandon the law for some time now, won't you?"

"I am going to apply for a position with the Museum," he answered. "Field work. I really would like to do it. I can always go back and try to work up a practice in law again. But this sort of thing—this is the work I love."

"And how successful you have been at it already!" said Pollyanna. "I shouldn't think you'd have any trouble at all getting your position."

"We've all been lucky," he replied.

"And I'm most lucky of all, that nothing has happened to any of you," said Pollyanna thankfully.

"I believe I know what happened to Miss Aguamonte's father," said Jimmy. "Because the same sort of thing happened again, and made it possible for us to find the mine, and get into the mountain. There are often little quakes up there. I felt several I did not mention. Three came one evening, just as we were eating, that broke off loose ledges, and sent them down in landslides, revealing to us, when we looked the next day, the opening of one of the old tunnels, and also a bit of the wall that surrounds the pyramid. I believe that in that mountain there has always been a great natural stone cave, which some ancient people made use of as a ceremonial place. The pyramid was built inside there, and some sort of funeral services were held, for there are heaps of stones that must have been graves, and some coffers still complete standing about.

"Water must have burrowed out that cave origi-
nally. There is still an underground stream in there
—I heard it, but could not see it. The quakes shift
it about. Poor Aguamonte must have got caught
inside there once in a bad quake, when the stream
burst out of its bed and through into the tunnels of
the mine the Spaniards started. Curiously enough,
there is ore, good ore, and plenty of it, on the other
side of the mountain. Apparently the great cave,
the graves and the pyramid were unsuspected by the
workers of the mine. But the Indians up there must
have known about the cave and the graves all the
time. Curious people. Secretive."

"No," said Pollyanna. "Just afraid, probably."

"What does it all look like?" asked Pollyanna.
"The pyramid, I mean, and the graves, and the
cave. . . ."

"Our flares were pretty good at first," said Jimmy.
"We used too many of them, in our excitement, and
had to cut down later.

"Aguilar had found a sort of wall, stones laid
close together, fitted,—a man-made thing. Then,
as he worked clearing it away, some carving showed.
We knew it must be something ancient, something
marvelous.

"But, as chance had it, we gave up digging along
his wall, to free it from the mountain, from the

outside, and went along the tunnels that I had found
opened up by another of those landslides. It was a
simple, quite steep tunnel, and we passed some of
the old workings. It's a good mine still—not half
mined out.

"Suddenly I came to a place where a great lot of
rocks and beams from the tunnel wall had been
shaken down, and there was another tunnel, bursting
straight out of the mine shaft, and this tunnel is lined
with carefully cut stones, dark gray, with pink vein-
ings, like the rocks Aguilar came across in the wall.

"There are little recessed places along this tunnel,
and urns are set in them. They may have contained
oil to burn, flowers—I don't know.

"Well, here and there as you walk along the
stones are damp, and clammy, and you can faintly
hear water—somewhere inside.

"I don't remember how long that tunnel is—how
long did we figure it to be, Aguilar?—but we later
decided that it probably led to the exact center of
the mountain. And it seems to be exactly in the
center that there is this stony cave—enormous, and
damp, with a sound of water never out of hearing.
And inside the cave, not in the dead center of it, but
extending backward into the solid mountain is a
pyramid of stone, with a sort of altar on top. And
instead of stairs going up the exact center of one

of the walls, the stairs ascend on either side of great
stone doorways, closed tight, in the middle.

"Ranged round that sort of hall,—the cave looks
like one, and gives the general impression of one,
are casket-like boxes of stone. The quakes had jarred
some of them—one had been knockd to bits some
time ago, and was strewn over the cave-floor,—
spilled out jewelry, golden masks, earrings of jade—
such stuff as you never dreamed of. And some
quake, whether this one or some older one, had
opened one of the stone doors of the pyramid a little
—not enough to be of help to us, but enough to let
us see definitely that it was never meant to be mor-
ticed up.

"Have I said enough?"

"Oh, Jimmy, it's too fantastic."

"Tomorrow, after Junior has developed some of
his films, you'll see something! I'm no good at de-
scribing anything!"

"Junior, were you in the cave?"

"Yes, I was, Mama."

And at the wonder that leapt into his eyes at the
mention of it, she knew that this fairy tale was real,
as real as that other discovery at Monte Alban. . . .

"Well, it's a land of miracles," she said at last
weakly. "Mexico is wonderland."

CHAPTER XXII

THE PARTY

THE first of the summer rains had fallen in the afternoon,—a sudden darkening of the sky, and rushing of water down from the clouds, and then blue satin above as fresh and clean as if it had just been bought off a store counter.

Then the sun came out, warm and golden, and the hours dripped away until sunset, like honey off a spoon—slow, golden, and sweet.

Everything had been done inside the little pink house. The tiles of the floors had been washed in the morning, and everything dusted and set to rights. Fresh candles glimmered softly in colored glass cups in niches along the walls, fresh flowers stood up straight and fragrant from vases everywhere, and the patio had been watered twice, so that every green leaf glistened and there was a sweet dampish smell like fern and dew among the rose bushes.

In the kitchen all was in readiness. Pollyanna herself had got the chickens ready for roasting, American-style, and had made a savory stuffing for

them. They were ready to be put into the ovens at
five o'clock, and Lolita now watched the clock for
the time to start them baking. The vegetables were
prepared and waiting, the salad was made; ingred-
ients for hot biscuits stood ready for Pollyanna's
hand—these were to be mixed and baked at the last
minute—and the chocolate cake, light and rich, and
luscious with a thick chocolate frosting, sat black and
important on its serving dish.

Pollyanna had bathed, and was resting in her ki-
mono, reviewing in her mind all the preparations.
She heard the gentle plodding to and fro of Lolita,
who was setting the table in the tiled, open hall near
the patio. Ruth and Judy had been bathed, and
dressed in fresh underwear. They were now getting
into their dresses—the new party dresses!—and
Judy was to comb Ruth's hair and her own, and affix
their bright new hair-ribbons.

Now came a yodelling from the bathroom. Jimmy
and Junior were at their ablutions.

Pollyanna thought a moment longer: The bells
from the cathedral sang a slow song as the shadows
lengthened outside the iron-barred windows of the
little pink house.

"Everything is ready," she concluded at last, and
then suddenly her eyes filled with tears, and she
could not prevent them from slipping over. "How

Nancy would have loved being here," she thought,
"quietly part of the preparations and the festivities.
How she would have loved watching the children
dress, and combing their hair, and fussing at me to
hurry. Oh, Nancy, now that you've been gone some
weeks, I miss you more than ever. I keep listening
for your step and your voice, as if you had been
away, and should be home again now. . . ."

She turned over and hid her face in the pillow, and
it was there that Jimmy found her.

"Hoity, toity!" he clucked, "as the duchess would
say. Tears? Darling, what's the matter?"

He put a finger under her chin, and made her turn
her flushed, tear-wet face to his. He laid his cheek
against hers. He was freshly shaved, and he smelled
fragrant of bay rum and shaving powder.

"Don't cry, honey. She's here, really. With you,
where she always loved to be."

Pollyanna said nothing, but she pressed her cheek
against his gratefully. After a moment she got up,
dusted her face with powder, and began brushing her
hair. Then she slipped into her blue lace dress. It
was not a new dress, nor particularly stylish, but it
looked like Pollyanna. It was simply cut, and long,
and gently flowing around her as she walked, and
the blue of it was the blue of her eyes,—shining and
kind.

"My favorite dress," smiled Jimmy at her, into the mirror.

Pollyanna's spirits were reviving quickly. She began to glow with expectation.

"The Morenos will be so happy that you are home. It would have been too bad if you hadn't been here to say Goodbye to Ramon before he went to the states."

"I'm glad, too," said Jimmy. "And I'm glad he has been invited. He deserves those honors. The road is a great achievement, and to Ramon should go much of the credit."

Pollyanna gave a last look at herself. Smooth shining hair, pink cheeks, the long sweep of the blue gown. All right. Then she went into the girls' room.

Judy, in her new dress, with her dark curls wet from a recent combing, was brushing Ruth's silken yellow hair into bangs, and tying on a big pink ribbon. Ruth sat with bated breath, hoping, as she always did, that when her hair was done, and when she finally looked into the mirror, she would see a vision of slender loveliness,—like Judy. Judy finished, and Ruth rushed to look, the wish still hopefully radiant in her round eyes. But no. The mirror said what it always did. It said that Ruth was round and brown, that her hair was straight and yellow, and her cheeks pink as apples, and that her eyes were round as blue marbles, and that freckles marched across her small nose.

"You look nice, my dears!" said Pollyanna. "Come now. I've aprons for you. You must help me."

Lolita had spread the white cloth on the big table, and had set out the beautiful heavy earthenware Mexican dishes,—brown and blue, and gre a—and had laid out the silver, and the bubbly amethyst Guadalajara glass.

Pollya na gave Judy scissors and sent her into the patio to cut flowers for the table.

"Get blue lilies, and purple ones," she said, "and some pink roses. Ruthie, put the napkins around, and arrange the knives and forks this way. Mama will show you."

Ruth's tongue protruded, so intent was she on doing everything correctly.

Then the knocker sounded, and Pollyanna whisked off her apron, and went to the door.

It was the Morenos, smiling on the doorstep, their arms loaded with flowers. Anita, in a starchy white dress, with a big white hair-ribbon, proferred a bunch of pansies, Mrs. Moreno gave carnations, and Mr. Moreno sweet peas. Señor Bello, who was with them, tendered another bunch of carnations.

"But I'm overcome!" cried Pollyanna. "Four

bunches of flowers! Such lovely ones." She buried her face in the velvety sweet-smelling pansies.

"We've been to Xochimilco," said Anita.

"Ah," said Pollyanna. "The floating gardens! Now I know where all these beautiful flowers came from."

"It was Señor Bello," said Mrs. Moreno, "who suggested that we meet an hour and a half before coming here to you, and that we go out to the floating gardens, and buy you some flowers from the canoes."

"I love them," said Pollyanna. "Come in, all of you. I am so happy that you can be with us. And Jimmy and Junior are home!"

"Splendid!" said Mr. Moreno, and his face lighted with pleasure.

Pollyanna took the hats and jackets into the cloak-room, and then rejoined her guests in the living room. Jimmy came in, hearty and merry, and Ramon Moreno clapped him on the back with the left hand, as he shook hands with the right, in the Mexican fashion.

The three men were dressed in light summer suits, and Mrs. Moreno and Anita both wore white, though not the same kind of white, for Anita's dress stood out around her small body like the stiff petals of a flower, while Mrs. Moreno's dress fell in long soft ruffles of chiffon to her ankles.

"Ruth," said Pollyanna to the little girl, as she emerged from the dressing room where she left the hats and coats, "Anita is here, and she has brought flowers. Judy! Judy dear! There are flowers and more than enough!"

Anita had come out, looking for Judy and Ruth, and now she had found them, and they all started toward the kitchen to get vases and glasses and bowls into which to put the flowers from Xochimilco.

"What is Xochimilco?" asked Judy of Anita.

"It's a place where there are many many rivers and canals and little lakes," said Anita, "and there are trees around, and flower gardens. Everything is green and lovely, and the Indians will take you out on the water in little canoes, or little boats with covers across them to keep the sun out of your eyes. And then others come by in little boats and sing and play to you, and still others come with their boats full of flowers. Like these."

In the living room, Jimmy, Mr. Moreno and Señor Bello were talking roads. Señor Bello, though a musician, was tremendously interested in all practical schemes for the opening up of Mexico so that tourists could see for themselves the beauties of his country.

"Señor Bello is a patriot—a poetic patriot," said

Mr. Moreno. "He has a scheme for building character through music. . . ."

"Really?" asked Jimmy, interested. "May I hear it? Or would a musical amateur like me be able to understand it?"

"It is a simple plan," said Señor Bello, happy to be talking about one of his favorite projects. "We are beginning, in the earliest grades, to train the children to rhythm,—to inspiring, active, exuberant rhythms. It sets the pace of work, keys up thinking. We allow no tiresomely sentimental tunes, no tearful dirges, no songs with anything but a fine vigorous rhythmical life, and a melody that expresses hope and accomplishment."

"I don't see why your scheme might not work very well," said Jimmy, "but I think you have to count on physical health and many other factors, too."

"Of course," said Señor Bello. "But for some extraordinary reason we seldom start teaching our children the best music. We let their childish ears grow used to poor harmonic progressions, to poorly built and sickly tunes, to infantile poetry. No wonder many of them grow into adult perceptions without ever learning how to appreciate good music. It would be the same thing if we trained our children to read on poorly written stories and poetry that limped."

While Mrs. Moreno helped put finishing touches on the table, Pollyanna went into the kitchen and got her biscuits ready for the oven. And then she set Lolita to making tiny little hot-cakes, into each of which she spooned a scrap of jelly.

It wasn't long before the two families and Señor Bello sat down at the long table to Pollyanna's American farewell dinner. Flowers were tucked into everyone's napkin; the men put theirs into their buttonholes. Pollyanna passed hers through the mesh of the lace in the bosom of her dress. Mrs. Moreno put hers in her hair.

Lolita served the fruit cocktail first.

Then the chickens came on the table to be carved, and Pollyanna's fluffy white biscuits, and the tiny pancakes, that made Mrs. Moreno scream with joy, "Hot cakes! American hotcakes!"

While everyone was eating merrily, and Lolita was passing biscuits, suddenly the bells of the cathedral burst into a sweet wild clangor. Jose was playing—and it was a new song. One he had never played before. Though the Pendleton's had heard the bells many times a day, they all stopped to listen. The Moreno's were silent. And Señor Bello stopped

still, and then he began to smile . . . a smile of sheer
enjoyment.

It was a wild, exuberant sound, full of a mysterious melody, sweet and yet a little sad, too, as if the
player sang of expectation that another day was coming, rather than quiet joy at the one just passed.

When the overtones had all faded into silence, and
the song was ended, Señor Bello said, quietly, as if
thinking aloud, "I have never heard such music—
such personal music—from church bells before. An
interesting carilloneur."

Pollyanna turned to Señor Bello with shining eyes.

"I'd like you to meet the carilloneur, Señor Bello.
I have asked him to come in for a moment. He will
join us at dessert."

"I'm delighted," said the musician.

"And so am I," said Mrs. Moreno. "The music
was glorious."

"I warn you! You'll be surprised," said Pollyanna.

Ruth looked up curiously.

"Why will Jose surprise them, Mama?"

"Jose?" echoed Mr. Moreno. "It sounds as if
this bell-player were a very good friend indeed."

"He's Judy's beau," said Ruth.

"Ruthie!"

But Judy's flush of anger and embarrassment went unnoticed, for just then the doorbell rang.

"Let me go, Mama," said Ruth, getting down from her chair, napkin still attached inside the collar of her dress. "I bet that's Jose."

"All right, Ruthie. And send Lolita to bring another chair, and another service when she brings the dessert."

"You see," said Pollyanna, turning to Señor Bello, "our carilloneur is only twelve years old. He is thrilled to have the opportunity to meet you. Was I wrong to promise it to him even before I asked you?"

"I think that the opportunity is mine," said Señor Bello. "He must be a very talented boy."

CHAPTER XXIII

JUDY AND JOSE

JOSE came in modestly. He was nicely dressed though his clothes were poor, and there shone in his dark face an expectant happy light.

Señor Bello rose from the table, and extended his hand.

"I am Ignacio Bello, of the Conservatory," he said. "I am delighted to meet you. I'd like to talk with you about your music."

Jose shook hands gravely, "Jose Revilla. At your service."

Then Jose went to where Pollyanna sat, and greeted her. He greeted everyone before he would sit, where Lolita stood ready, holding his chair.

"Chocolate cake for everyone," called Pollyanna gaily, and standing up in order to cut the big brown cake, she sank the knife into its creamy richness.

Over the cake the conversation grew gay and loud. Everyone was talking. Jimmy and Ramon Moreno were talking college days again, Mrs. Moreno was talking about art with Judy, Anita and Ruth had a

257

little conversation of their own, and Pollyanna listened happily to what Señor Bello was telling Jose.

"Have you ever had any formal lessons in music?"

"Yes. My father has taught me how to read music, and how to write down the music I make up."

"You compose, then?"

"I think of tunes and harmonies that I wish to
hear, and then I try them, and I write them. But I
know that that is not composing. I only try."

"Was that your own—what you just now played?"

Señor Bello had removed his horn-rimmed glasses,
and held them in his hand. He was looking at the
boy kindly and interestedly. Pollyanna saw the boy's
profile flush a little with joy, to know that the great
musician of Mexico was thus talking to him, like a
friend, like a co-worker. Pollyanna realized as she
looked at Jose, how handsome he was, and how much
more handsome he was going to be. The line of the
nose was spirited, delicately aquiline, with nostrils
that betrayed intensity and vigor, the mouth finely
modeled and sensitive, the chin strong, and the eyes,
under heavy level brows, proud, intelligent, warm.

Both had forgotten their cake. It lay under their
idle forks, melting a bit at the edges, and the coffee
grew cold in their cups, but Pollyanna did not mind.
Her happiness lay in bringing things together that

need each other, and she knew that Jose needed help such as Bello would be able to give.

Finally Pollyanna gave the signal to leave the table. The stars were out now, and a moon was rising. Already the patio was silvery in its beams. They all sat in the garden, Pollyanna and Mrs. Moreno carrying their coffee cups with them. Presently the glow of the men's cigarettes described little arcs in the shadowy dark as they raised their hands to their mouths, and took in breaths of fragrant smoke.

Señor Bello and Jose were quietly talking on a bench. Presently Jose got up, shook hands and thanked Señor Bello, and then came to Pollyanna to wish her goodnight, and make his farewells.

Pollyanna excused herself from her guests in order to accompany Jose to the door.

"I have asked Lolita to make a package of a piece of the cake for your father," she said, dropping her arm across the boy's slender shoulders as they walked. "I would have liked to have him come to dinner with us tonight, but I know that for him to go up and down the stairs is so difficult, and not worth anything merely social like this."

"Oh, this was not merely social, or merely anything, for me," said Jose quickly. "This was wonderful. Señor Bello has asked me to come to the

Conservatory tomorrow to talk with him and some of the teachers. He says he believes he can arrange for me to study with the best in Mexico, and perhaps some day—some day! they may even send me to Spain, to hear the bells, and to France!"

"Jose! I'm so happy for you!"

"Ah, how I will study. How I will work!"

Judy came shyly and stood by her mother.

Jose turned toward her and seized her hands and swung them.

"You will see, Judy! Some day you will be proud of me!"

"We are proud of you already," said Judy.

"Come and tell me what Señor Bello says to you tomorrow, after you have seen him, will you, Jose?"

"Yes, I will. And thank you, for everything."

Lolita came, smiling, with a package of cake in her hand. Jose accepted it gratefully, and then quickly left. His steps were as light as if he had wings to his heels, and Pollyanna's heart felt the same.

"How good you are, Mama. You may have given Jose something that may be the beginning of his life."

"It would have come to him anyway, I'm sure, if it was meant to be," said Pollyanna gravely. "But I hope I may have helped."

The party talked in the patio for some hours.
Addresses were exchanged, and cards to friends.
Then at last, all the farewells were said, and the
kisses and handshakes of Goodbye were given.

The Morenos and Señor Bello went away in a
taxi, and the Pendletons did not see them again for
many months——until the Morenos had finished their
tour of the East, and were homeward bound again.
But that is another story.

"Well," said Jimmy to Pollyanna, after the children had been sent to bed, and they were discussing
the party between themselves in the quiet patio for
a moment. "There goes one of the best fellows I
know, and a great engineer. I hope we meet soon
again."

* * * * * * *

Pollyanna and Jimmy went to tea at the Geneve
Hotel the next day, to meet the proprietors of the
hotel, a charming couple, who were friends of the
Morenos——Mr. and Mrs. Thomas Gore, whose hotel
was the great rendezvous for Americans in Mexico
City.

Junior was busy developing his films in the bathroom, improvised into a dark room, and with strict
orders given to everyone not to open either of the

bedroom doors, for fear a streak of light might creep in, and spoil the precious films.

Ruth, washed clean, trotted away to market with Lolita, happily clinging to Lolita's brown hand.

Judy, alone in the house, had been writing a letter to Myra Britton, her Hollywood dancing teacher, who had done much to give the confused artistic longings of the little girl a direction and an impetus.

After she had re-read and sealed the letter, Judy sat at the table, thinking about those happy hours in the school, tip-toe by the bar, feeling her muscles stretch and strengthen, feeling her body poised as if on invisible wires from above, feeling the rhythm of music throb through her, and lift her into motion.

She sighed, and a wave of homesickness flowed over her—for the things she used to do, old friends, familiar faces. She felt her tears rise, and her breath catch.

There was the sound of the knocker and the door-bell at once. Judy went to the door slowly, and looked out before she opened it, for she was alone in the house, and her mother had warned her never to let anyone in who was a stranger, when she was alone.

But as she looked out, her tears dried in her eyes, if not on her cheeks, and she threw open the door gladly. It was Jose.

He stepped into the hallway, his face radiant with good news.

"Judy! I am to study with Señor Bello himself! Every day! He will teach me theory and piano first, and every day I can go to the conservatory to practice! And then, some day . . . to Spain. Maybe with him!"

"Oh Jose, how wonderful!"

They went into the patio and sat down. It was then, when he saw the sunlight on her face, that he saw the signs of tears.

"Crying? Only the other day Ruth was crying! Why are you sad?"

"I was thinking about dancing school, and my teacher . . . I love to dance, and it is so long since I did."

"Well, don't cry! I will teach you a Mexican dance! You never did one of them at your dancing school, did you?"

"No, I didn't. Could you really, Jose? Where did you learn it?"

"Just watching. That's how we all learn. At school, when I was very little, we all danced in the school yard. And then, at the markets sometimes, you can see people dancing. And during the big fiestas, they dance in the streets. Everyone has such a gay time! Look, here is how you stand to start."

He jumped up and took a position, his hands clasped in back, his body leaning forward a little from the waist.

Judy was quick. The steps were such fun! So quick and so merry. Jose sang the tune that they danced to. By the end of an hour they were warm, and their hair clung to their damp foreheads in moist ringlets.

"Now do it alone," commanded Jose. "I will sing."

And Judy flicked back her skirts, tossed her head, and danced the steps he had taught her, laughing as she did.

"Brava, brava!" He took her by the shoulders, and gave her a loud boyish kiss.

"You are my sweetheart," he said.

"Oh Jose," said Judy. "I think you are so wonderful."

"No, I am not. You are."

"Well, I am glad you like me."

"I love you. Some day I will marry you."

"Oh yes. Yes!" said Judy.

*   *   *   *   *   *   *

"Oh, I am sorry Jose has been here, and has gone,

already," said Pollyanna, coming into the house with
pink cheeks from a merry ride back from the tea with
a party of friends. "I wanted to hear all about what
Señor Bello said to him."

"He is going to teach Jose himself—piano and
theory—and Jose is to practice every day on a piano
at the Conservatory," told Judy breathlessly, "and
some day Señor Bello promised to take him to Spain."

Jimmy whistled.

"The boy must have the real stuff in him," commented Jimmy. "Hello! Here's Junior, out of the
dark room. How did they come out, old fellow?"

Junior was jubilant.

"They're swell, Dad. Only two of them pretty
badly overexposed. I forgot to allow for the greater
brilliance of mountain light. But mother will be able
to see what we found all right. I'm going to call up
Mr. Aguilar, mother, may I, and ask him to come
over. I know he'll want to see the pictures."

"Yes, do call him up."

The evening was a memorable one for Pollyanna.

Junior's excellent pictures, revealing discoveries
that were to make Señor Aguilar's name and her
husband's almost household words in Mexico, and
the maturity of her boy's comments on what he had
seen and photographed—the comradely way in which

he shared the conversation with her husband and Señor Aguilar awoke Pollyanna to the fact that Junior was rapidly becoming a man.

And his confidence to her, after Aguilar had gone, having asked to be allowed to take the negatives of the pictures and have enlargements made of all of them, made her realize the fact that he was now capable of taking a course of action without having previously consulted her.

"I sent a couple of pictures into a contest, mother. If I get any award, I should be hearing it pretty soon. I'd like to win one."

"What were your subjects?"

"I sent two—one of some hats, as they were being tossed into the bull-ring. . . ."

"Junior! You didn't go to a bull fight? You never told me."

"Well, yes, I did mother. To get material for pictures. I didn't think it would upset you."

"I'd rather you let me know your plans in advance instead of afterward."

"I'm sorry, mother! I wanted to surprise you!"

"Well, never mind. Don't always surprise me though."

And then Judy's whispered confidence.

"Mother, I'm engaged."

"Judy. Don't be foolish. You're only a little girl."

"But mother, Jose says he wants to marry me some day."

"Some day is a long way off."

"But I love him, Mother. Couldn't I marry him when I'm—when I'm sixteen?"

"You'd better not think about getting married at all, for years and years," said Pollyanna, somewhat sharply.

"It won't be long before I'm sixteen," protested Judy softly.

"It will be a long long time before I want to hear you discussing marriage with any one," said Pollyanna. "You're just a baby, and you mustn't be so romantic. It isn't becoming. Haven't you been ashamed at what Ruthie has said? Ruthie notices how you make romance out of everything. You must get over it, and be a sensible little girl. I've been patient with you, but this is too much."

"Mother," said Judy, a little sadly, "I don't think I'll ever be really sensible, do you?"

And Pollyanna, startled and dismayed for a moment, had realized that she didn't think so either.

CHAPTER XXIV

AT THE MINE. THIEVES FROM THE AIR

JIMMY and Junior and Mr. Aguilar stopped at the little town where they got their men and burros and supplies for the trip across the sierra to the mine. They were full of eagerness to get back again, to carry their work forward. The government was sending an official to pronounce on it within four days, and an appointee from the museum was coming, at the same time, to appraise the treasures already found, and to advise about packing them.

But after a few conversations, in Spanish, with the Indians who had gone with them before, and then with others, Señor Aguilar returned to Jimmy and Junior, pale and agitated.

"Something has happened," he said. "I can't quite get to the bottom of it, but they seem unwilling to pack us in again. And there is some sort of a cock and bull story about thieves."

"Why, we've got to have men," said Jimmy. "Offer them more. Or do something. There must be one of them—that fellow who was such a help

inside the mine, the only one who would go in, you
remember—there must be one of them who can
elaborate this story."

Junior was worried. "What the dickens . . . ?
Nobody but those Indians knew what was in the
mountains," he said. "How could there have been
any thieves. The Indians themselves couldn't sell
any of those things without arousing suspicion. . . ."

Aguilar came back with a worried face. "I've got
two who promise to come along," he said. "The story
seems to be definitely that there was a theft. Out of
the air. You don't suppose. . . ."

"An airplane? That's possible. But it seems
fantastic."

"The thing that makes it bad," said Aguilar, "and
the reason why we can't get any more men, is that
the two men that were left to guard the mine while
the others came back down here for some sort of
fiesta, have disappeared. One of those who went back
from the fiesta a little before the rest, saw an airplane
flying overhead, and he swears that he believes the
two men who disappeared went away in it."

"Queer business," said Jimmy. "Well, nothing to
do now but get into the valley as fast as we can."

The trip across the mountains seemed inordinately
slow. The men were impatient and pale and jumpy.
The two Indians who had agreed to supply burros

and make camp for them were silent, and serious.
They acted scared, and would say little.

It was nearing sundown when the little cavalcade
descended into the valley of the Mountain of Death.
Long purplish shadows were drifting down from
the peaks and falling across the valley floor. The
lake sparkled mysteriously, a deep blue, still, but as
if a diamond within it were sending up shafts of
brilliance through the water.

"Nothing to do before morning," said Jimmy,
after they had pitched camp. It was dark now, and
the stars were rising.

The three men shook hands silently, and went to
bed. A restless sleep fell on them.

*   *   *   *   *   *   *

It was Junior who woke first, after all, just as
the dawn broke, and who saw what was happening.

He called his father, but silently.

"Dad! Dad!" He shook his father, who was still
huddled in his blankets, gently snoring.

"Hm? Oh, Hello. What time is it?"

"Dad, come on. There's an airplane circling, and
getting ready to land."

"That's so?" Jimmy was awake and out of his
blankets in a twinkling.

"Get Aguilar," he commanded. "No, I'll call him. You stay still. If they notice us moving around they may not land."

And he yelled "Aguilar! Wake up!"

But it didn't take his voice to awaken Aguilar. The roar of the motor of the descending plane had him out of his bed in a moment.

"They're going to make a landing on the lake," shouted Aguilar. "They're landing!"

Jimmy, Aguilar, and Junior ran over to the shores of the lake, and watched the plane settle gently on the water, and then taxi over to the shore.

A man in flying togs got out, and marched up to the three defiantly.

"Just who are you?" he asked curiously. "Muscling in on my stuff?"

"What do you mean?" asked Jimmy. "What stuff?"

"My mine here."

The man, who was young, but whose face was hard as granite, and scarred, whipped a revolver out of his pocket, and covered the three.

"Hands up!" he snapped.

Junior and Aguilar did as they were told. Jimmy raised his hand a little more slowly.

"What's the meaning of this?" he asked pleasantly. "You come down out of the air, and land here on

the lake, and hold us up. What for? We've got
nothing you'd want except some beans and
chocolate."

The man's eyes traveled shiftily from one to the
other, but he still kept his gun in place.

"I don't want you around here," he said. "I've
got work to do."

"What work? Maybe we could help you?"

"I ought to bump you off, all three of you, right
now," said the man, slowly, to himself. His airplane
bobbed gently on the water behind him.

Then he caught sight of the two Indians, hurrying
away toward the mountain.

He shifted his gun and it spat fire. The earth
leaped in a little streak near one of the Indians.
"Come on over here or I'll shoot you," bawled the
man to the two. They came silently, not too fast.

"Tie these fellows up," commanded the man with
the gun, and he said something else to them in
Spanish, though he was obviously not a Mexican.

Jimmy, Aguilar, and Junior severely trussed up
and propped, like three sacks of meal against a tree,
the man sent the two Indians ahead of him, still
keeping his gun trained on them, and started quickly
for the opening in the mountain.

Aguilar called to Jimmy, when the man had got
out of sight.

"We might have overpowered him, Pendleton, if we'd both jumped on him, but I was afraid there'd be a shot or two, and I wouldn't jeopardize the boy."

"I'm glad you didn't," said Jimmy. "This is our thief all right, and something tells me that I'm going to remember where I've seen his face before, too. Can you move at all, Aguilar?"

"No."

Jimmy struggled until the sweat burst from every pore, but he couldn't dislodge a single rope or raw-hide riata.

"Nothing to do but wait," said Jimmy, at last, and he was right.

While the sun climbed up along the blue circle of the arched sky, while gnats bothered them, and their skin parched, and they longed for water, all three had to lie there and wait, furious, trapped, uncomfortable, and impatient.

Junior spoke at last.

"I have been trying to figure out how he would know to stop here unless he knew about the mine, Dad," he said. "I've got a funny feeling he must have seen something in the lake, from above. Look. That plane isn't a regular aqua-plane. It has been fixed up with pontoons recently."

"I believe you're right, kid."

Junior's words were proved. It may have been

about three when the two Indians, burdened with
gold vessels and vases, came stumbling ahead of the
man back down the mountain.

He gave a snarling look at the three, and tested
their bonds himself, the muzzle of his gun pressed
against their sides as he grudgingly proved to himself that they were still unable to move without pain.
Under the tight bonds already their flesh had swollen
and was red and ugly with clotted circulation.

Then he took the gold from the Indians and himself stowed it away inside his plane. Shivering and
scared the two Indians tried to run, but the gun
spoke again, and they came to heel like frightened
dogs.

Then the man made the Indians get into his plane,
got in himself, and wheeled it round and taxied it
carefully into what seemed to be the exact center of
the lake.

Then he let down into the water, from his pilot's
compartment, leaning out, and working carefully,
a sort of deep, weighted dredge. Blop! It fell into
the water, and then gurgled downward. The man
swept it around, and then at last he brought it up.
The three tied on the bank saw something golden and
glittery. He dragged again and again. Six times
in all he dragged about on the lake bottom with his

improvised sweep, and each time the sun sparkled off yellow metal.

Then, with a satirical wave of the hand to the three who sat round-eyed at what he had dredged up from the lake, he started the great motors of his plane, taxied it down the lake, and then began to lift, and to circle.

But before any one of the three could say a word, or emit an epithet of disappointment and rage, something happened!

The airplane began to waver, to drop, and to labor to pick itself up and into the air again. Then suddenly, and in less time than it takes to tell, it bent on its side, and rushed roaring to the earth, and flames flowed from it like the tail of a comet. It struck the side of the mountain, crashed and crumbled, and pieces of it rolled down the mountain.

"I wish I could cross myself," said Aguilar. "Our Indians are dead."

"And he is dead," said Junior.

"God! That's an awful thing to see happen, even to a desperado like Cutler. I remember that man. It's Dan Cutler— There are rewards out for him everywhere. Both our countries are better off with him out of the way."

"But we've got to get loose," suddenly jerked out

Junior. "How can we, Dad? Think of some way!"
The boy's voice was close to hysteria. The whole
day had been an ordeal and a shock.

"If I can wriggle myself over near the fire," said
Jimmy, "I can burn off the rope around my wrists,
I think. There must be some coals still. . . ."

It was hard. It took exactly three hours. Every
muscle and bone in Jimmy's body ached. But he
made it. And though he burned himself badly, he
got his hands free.

Junior, for all he was so close to manhood, was
crying like a little boy of three, when his father
finally cut his bonds loose.

CHAPTER XXV

THE WRECK

"Poor souls," said Jimmy, as he and Aguilar looked at the mass of charred and broken timber and metal that had been a proud bird of the air.

"They hadn't a chance," said Aguilar.

They had made Junior stay behind and rest at camp. There could be nothing for the boy but shock and distress at the task that the two men now set themselves to.

It was not quickly done. It was in fact, mid-afternoon, when they rested from their labors, and when the last rude cross had been set up against the mute mound, which testified to any who might pass by that one of God's creatures had been garnered back into the soil which bears and nourishes and rests us all.

After they had started the tramp back to where Junior waited at camp, Aguilar and Jimmy discussed what had happened.

"He must have hidden away what he took that first trip, somewhere," said Aguilar. "From what he carried away this time, I doubt if he could have made any really noticeable holes in the bulk of the treasure. But it looks pretty certain that we ought to stick right here on guard until the government men arrive. This fellow may have confederates."

"I doubt it," said Jimmy, as he swished along through knee-high ferns and wild-flowers.

"I believe he was known as a lone wolf among crooks," he went on. "He was wanted in the states on many counts—usually daring robberies, and he wasn't above murder either. He had been a flier in the war. I had no idea he worked with a plane. But he was smart. I guess he may have figured out that he could do quite a bit of thieving just by cruising around and robbing historic places of unguarded treasures that would bring him more money and less danger than sticking up banks. There must be a big cache of his loot somewhere."

"Probably not in Mexico," said Aguilar.

"No, probably not," agreed Jimmy. "He was always too clever to dispose of his loot anywhere near where he got it. Since he has a plane, I dare say he has his stuff hidden in some republic to the south."

"Well, we will soon see how much he has taken from the mine," said Aguilar.

They were weary. After their experience of the

day before, they tired easily. They decided, when they had reached the lake again, and started the walk back to camp around the edge of it, to explore the mine the next day, and to finish out this one lolling at the shore, and turning in early. It would be another day or two before they could expect the government men or the representatives of the museum. anyway.

The lake sparkled a deep blue, and swished gently against the reeds and rocks that bordered it.

"We have Dan Cutler to thank for the definite proof of treasures in the lake," said Jimmy. "We had better put in our time making some sort of raft, so that we can go out to the center and explore further ourselves. There must be a lot of metal in the lake, to have attracted Cutler from the air."

"It would shine like a mirror, even from inside the water, at certain times of the day," said Aguilar.

They found Junior asleep. The boy had slept most of the day, because he had been unable to sleep, with pain from the bonds he had worn, and from excitement, the night before.

The next day they made their raft, and after some disappointment and search, they managed to dredge up a bar of metal.

"The lake isn't as deep as I thought it would be," said Jimmy. "I've got a notion to go down to the bottom and explore. I'll tie a rope around my middle, so that you can pull me up, Aguilar, if I'm down too long."

"The water is icy," warned Aguilar. "Are you sure you want to risk getting a chill? I'm not sure you should, up here, where it is high, and a cold is serious."

"Well, let's be thoughtful about it," said Jimmy. "Junior could have a good fire started on the shore to dry me out, and hot stuff ready to drink. And I could have blankets here on the raft to wrap up in. I've a good heart. If I can stand the immersion, I can stand a few minutes in the water. I want to try it."

"All right," said Aguilar.

That is how they discovered the other entrance to the cave inside the Mountain of Death.

For deep inside the lake, Jimmy found a long flight of steps, tiled and carefully made that led upward, upward, upward, and into a tunnel that ascended into the mountain, with water flowing along on either side, and all as black as night.

He could not ascend far, but it was far enough to give him an idea of how true Miss Aguamonte's suspicions were. Water and death in the mountain.

CHAPTER XXVI

HOME AGAIN. A LETTER

Jimmy, Junior, and Aguilar, returning to Mexico City with the government officials who had been sent to view their discoveries, and the museum representatives who had come to pronounce upon their authenticity, and to mark out for Jimmy the territory he might still legitimately open up for Miss Aguamonte as a gold mine, were met before they had got to Oaxaca by reporters and camera men.

The museum representative did much of the talking for the papers.

"It is undoubtedly one of the greatest archæological treasure-houses of our century," he said, while the busy reporter made extensive notes.

"The discoveries at Monte Alban only seem richer and more extensive. But this mountain, whether hollowed out by nature or by the people themselves who set up their temples of death there, and therein buried their illustrious dead, intrigues the imagination powerfully.

"There was one great entrance, from the base

281

of the mountain, by means of a tunnel along an
inner water-way. Earth shocks had changed the
course of the stream, and closed off that entrance,
and a lake, of fairly recent origin, has formed a
great pool which concealed that opening.

"A gold mine, for the mountain is rich in ore,
stumbled into the main tunnel into the cave, and
the tragedies which resulted when a small earthquake changed the course of the underground stream,
and sent some of it out into the mine tunnels, bursting
down the walls, and flooding the mine, plus the
ancient superstitions and ceremonies of the place,
have given it the Indian name of 'The Mountain of
Death.'

"James Pendleton, an American engineer working
for a Mexican citizen in rehabilitating and opening
the gold mine, and Juan Aguilar, a lawyer of this
city whose amateur explorations have led him to
this remarkable discovery, are jointly responsible
for the find.

"I confidently expect that officials of the museum,
as well as of the government, will honor these two
men, as well as Pendleton's young son, whose
excellent photographs of the finds in the original
condition in which they were found, will become
valuable museum property.

"It is as yet impossible to determine which of the

ancient nations of Mexico left the heritage of jewels,
of gold, carved jade and onyx, and stonework which
awaits in the temple of death the hand of collectors.
A heavy guard has been placed about the mine and
the vicinity, as well as the lake which conceals one
of the ancient entrances to the chamber of death
inside the mountain. Already one depredation, and
possibly two were made upon the treasures of the
mine by a man who flew into the valley in an airplane, had Pendleton, Aguilar and the boy bound,
and made their two Indian guides carry loot out of
the mine and stow it in his plane. Then he made
them get aboard with him. Pendleton and Aguilar
saw the plane crash, and I have myself seen its
wreckage, and the graves of the three men, for
after working himself loose from his bonds, Pendleton freed his companions, and he and Aguilar gave
the burned corpses from the plane decent burial."

Pollyanna put down the paper she was reading
and sat speechless.

This was the first news she had of her husband
and Junior since they had left for the mine. The
Mexico City papers were carrying the story on front
pages, with stream-line heads.

Pollyanna had been out shopping when she saw
the papers carrying headlines having to do with
something about "Americano."

She bought one, and tucked it under her arm, and
it was not until she had gone into Sanborn's, the
beautiful restaurant inside the famous old House of
Tiles, and had ordered one of their famous ices,
that she unfolded the paper, and began to read.

Immediately she saw the name Pendleton.

It took her some time to study out the story, for
her Spanish was not entirely dependable, but the gist
of it became clear after a few minutes, and she sat
there, petrified, while the deft waitress set a dish of
ice before her and said, in English, "Anything else,
madam?"

Pollyanna looked up, dazed.

"I see by the paper that my husband has just discovered a great treasure, and that a thief that tried
to take it away from him fell down in his airplane
and was burned to death," she said.

The waitress looked startled, and gave Pollyanna
a keen glance. "That so?" she asked suspiciously.

"Yes. No, I'm not crazy. I'm just surprised.
This is the first I've heard of it."

The waitress nodded, and Pollyanna had to smile
to herself to see the girl whispering excitedly with
the other waitresses back near the pastry counter at
the rear.

She finished her ice dreamily, thinking of the valley, the lake,—the wonders barely hinted at in the

newspaper account of the interview with the museum representative.

Suddenly she glanced at her watch.

"Why," she said, as the waitress came to gather up her emptied dish, "I must hurry home. The whole government may be waiting for me and my husband this minute, ready with a reception."

The girl gulped and hastily took Pollyanna's money and her charge ticket.

And as she hailed a taxi outside Pollyanna's eyes were bright with tears of suppressed laughter. "The girl is certain I'm crazy," she thought. "Maybe she's right."

She had not been at home ten minutes—had scarcely taken off her hat, and freshened her hair, and flicked a clean puff of powder over her nose, when she heard a commotion outside. She went to the window of her bedroom, opened the shutters, and looked out through the iron grilling.

Jimmy! and Junior! And Mr. Aguilar.

They were descending from an important-looking car, run by a chauffeur, and they were all leaning back into the car shaking hands with people. From another car piles of their luggage were being heaped on the sidewalk. Before she could get to the door Ruth and Judy had got there and opened it, and were being hugged and kissed. Mr. Aguilar tossed

Ruth into the air and caught her under the armpits, as if she were a small yellow sack of potatoes.

The excitement was noisy and gay! Junior talked constantly. Lolita began as a matter of course to set a bath running, and to lay a table in the patio.

When they were all gathered about that well-laden table some time later, the snatches of conversation did not fit into each other at all.

"Pollyanna, pass the pickles."

"Mother, Mr. Aguilar and Daddy helped bury that man, and the poor Indians he made go with them. What was that man's name, Daddy?"

"His name was,—I'm pretty sure of this, but I think it was Dan Cutler."

"Jimmy! Not that desperado—they've been making attempts to extradite him, and then couldn't find him. Not that fellow?"

"That's the one."

"Mr. Aguilar has an awful sunburn."

"Look at the marks from where I was tied up, Judy. Lookit."

"What's this in the papers about possibly getting some sort of government recognition? Jimmy, can you imagine? I was in Sanborn's, having an ice and read the whole thing in the paper."

The doorbell rang, but nobody heard it excep Lolita. And so great was the din that nobody sav her walk slowly past them all to the hall, and take a large white envelope from the boy who stood outside.

She tapped Jimmy on the shoulder twice, before he realized it, and turned. Then she simply proferred the envelope.

Suddenly a silence fell. All eyes were on that envelope.

"Read it to us, Jimmy," begged Pollyanna softly.

Jimmy looked around at the little group—Pollyanna and the two little girls wide-eyed with expectation, and Aguilar and Junior with peeling noses, sunburnt hair.

"Junior and I are to be received by the President of Mexico Wednesday at his home in San Angel," said Jimmy. "It's an honor."

"Well," said Aguilar, "I must rush home to get my envelope! I can't bear this adulation, if I don't get some of it!" And he laughingly rushed away.

"Oh Daddy," cried Ruth, "I bet you're going to get a medal!"

CHAPTER XXVII

THE PRESIDENT RECEIVES

JIMMY and Junior were ready. They were dressed in spotless white linen suits, and wore white shoes. Jimmy had a Panama. Junior wore no hat.

"Will there be any special etiquette to this, mother?" Junior had asked Pollyanna worriedly. She was laying out his clothes and seeing that everything was in order while he took his bath. He was dressed now, all except the tie, and he was taking time to that.

"I believe that this will be an extremely simple reception, dear," said Pollyanna. "Probably he will simply meet you, informally and pleasantly, chat with you, and then hurry on to some other important affairs. He is very busy, and he has never liked excessive formality, so they say. Like most distinguished people, he will soon make you forget that he is famous and powerful by making you like him so much that it doesn't matter. Just be yourself, and remember that good manners are simply thoughtfulness and courtesy magnified. I know you'll make me proud of you, and make the president glad he honored you with a personal visit."

"I guess I'm not important, anyway," said Junior. "It's Dad and of course Mr. Aguilar, that this is for."

"Yes," said Pollyanna, glad to encourage modesty in a young man, where it is most becoming.

"All ready, Kid?" Jimmy stood in the doorway of Junior's room, tall in his white suit, with the blue of his eyes startlingly light in his darkly tanned lean face.

"Okay, Dad."

Pollyanna saw them go, like each other in everything except years and height and the solidity of age.

"All I hope," she whispered to herself, as she watched the taxi drive away with them, "is that Junior isn't disappointed in this, his first public function. Somehow, I don't think he will be."

And then she sat down at her desk and drew out letter paper. Every one important to her should know about the honors that had come to her husband and her son in Mexico.

* * * * * * *

The taxi went down the main street of San Angel,

and then turned off on a side street, and bumped along cobble stones. On either side of the narrow street the walls of the houses formed a canyon down which cascaded purple-red bougainvillea, climbing rose, and honeysuckle.

Then, swinging round in a sort of small square, the taxi stopped in front of a great doorway, at least twelve feet square, and made of heavy wood studded with square nails, through which the automobile it-self might easily have driven.

"This must be a very old place," murmured Jimmy, as he heard the rattle and scrape of bars inside.

The door opened and they passed inside, into a tiled passage-way which opened onto an enormous garden—the most beautiful garden that Junior had ever seen. The patio seemed to be in two sections— there was an outer one beyond the one they looked into now, but here before them there were orange trees, and a fountain, and around the fountain, in pots, many red carnations, double, and filling the garden with spicy fragrance.

The yellow and dark blue gleam of a turret told them that there, at the far corner of the patio, was the private chapel.

But the servant was not taking them to the gar-den. He led them up some stairs and into a beau-

tiful reception room. There he took Jimmy's hat
and his invitation, and invited them to sit.

Junior sat in one of the great leather chairs.

"Gosh, Dad, what a beautiful house. What a
lovely place."

"Isn't it? I think so myself," said a tall man of
middle-age, boyish in spite of natural dignity, who
had entered unobserved.

"Do you know the president?" asked Junior.

"Quite well."

The tall man offered Jimmy cigarettes, and took
one himself.

"This house was in tumble-down-condition at
first," he said. "Look. The fireplace was put in
entirely new, and the ceiling was repaired. But the
old carving on the beams—that was there. And the
simple, hospitable, charming proportions. Don't
you like them? Come, let me show you through."

"Is it all right?" asked Junior. "We came here
to have tea with the president."

"The tea can wait a bit," said the tall man. "I
am the president."

"You?" Junior's jaw dropped, and the tall man
laughed heartily, but kindly. He clapped the boy on
the shoulder as if they were old friends.

"I suppose you thought I would have a drum play
and a trumpet call before I came in to meet you?" he

teased, his brown eyes twinkling, and his mustache rising at the corners of his mouth as he smiled.

"We were honored to be asked to come," said Jimmy, simply. "I'm Pendleton."

"I have asked Señor Aguilar, too," said the President, shaking Jimmy's hand heartily. "We must have a good informal talk. I went to college in the States for two years. My college licked yours at rowing. I almost made the rowing team, myself. Not quite, though."

The servant entered, quietly, and behind him walked Aguilar. The President strode over immediately to greet him.

"Come into my garden," said the President. "Beyond this little garden, we have my rose garden." And leading them across the small patio where the fountain splashed, he took them in a wide stretch of lawn and roses. Against the tall rose-colored walls grew cypress trees, and weeping willows, and under them there was a little table spread with a white cloth, and chairs were waiting.

"This was going to rack and ruin when I got it," said the President. "It has taken money and time to restore it for present day use, but I love the old things of our country better than some of the modern improvements—especially those of architecture —that you engineers are so busy inventing."

"I'm not an architectural engineer," said Jimmy. "I like the old things best myself."

"So I have noticed," said the President. "And so does Señor Aguilar."

"I am a lawyer," said Señor Aguilar. "I am an amateur archæologist only. It was luck—the good luck of meeting Señor Pendleton—which resulted in our finding the temple in the Mountain of Death."

"Well," said the President, ringing a little bell on the table, "you are all very modest. What is your excuse for the splendid pictures you took of those discoveries, young fellow?"

"A good camera," answered Junior.

The President's servant brought out cakes and tea, and sandwiches, and began deftly serving the four. The sun shone down through the green leaves above them, and a pattern moved gently on the white cloth. The scent of the roses, and of the hot fragrant tea which the President himself poured for his guests, mingled pleasantly. A big black cat came wandering across the green sun-lit lawn to rub itself affectionately against the President's trouser-leg. He lifted her into his lap immediately, and smoothed her fur with one hand, at which she settled her paws under her comfortably, and began to purr loudly.

"I would like very much to see this place you have found," said the President. "I have been an amateur archæologist myself. If I had not had so much time taken up by politics and the demands of my office, I might have found this myself. I am jealous of you. I cannot imagine anything I would like better than to look upon something with these living eyes of mine, that no other man's eyes had seen for endless centuries—to look upon history."

"Why couldn't you come up there and see it, before other people do?" suggested Junior.

"I wish I could. But I'm afraid I won't be able to."

The cakes and sandwiches were delicious. Junior forgot his shyness in the presence of a President, and began to discuss films with him. The President, it seemed, was a man who was interested in everything, and had tried a bit of everything.

"I think the museum is going to make you a handsome offer for your photographs," he said to Junior, pouring himself another cup of tea.

"If the museum would like to have my pictures," said Junior, "I will give them, not sell them."

The President's eyes lighted, and he shook Junior's hand impulsively.

"How generous of you! And you are at an age when boys like to feel the commercial value of their work. I appreciate what you have just said."

"It will be an honor for me to know that my pictures are in the museum," said Junior, and so earnest was he that he didn't even notice his father's proud eyes on him.

The President turned to Mr. Aguilar.

"And if you are willing to sacrifice your law practice for a time, Señor Aguilar, I believe you are going to be asked to head, with one other person, the excavating parties which will proceed with work, for the government and the museum, at the Mountain of Death."

"I could not wish for anything more," said Mr. Aguilar. "It is a work I love, and one I don't want to leave. But I wish to ask permission to use the name of Mr. James Pendleton as joint discoverer on all annotations, and in anything I may write on the subject."

"But of course that is expected—demanded," said the President.

"And Mr. Pendleton, I believe some worries you and your employer may have had about the continuance of work in the gold mine at the Mountain of Death, need trouble you no longer. Full permission to work the mine, under your employer's father's title to it, is granted, upon consultation with the excavating parties. We ask only that you cooperate thoroughly with the government explorations there, so that no treasures be lost or mutilated."

From such talk the conversation went to college days in the states, to archæology, to horses, to the history of the cat the president held in his lap, and to the news of the day.

When the President had finished his third cup of tea, all three took the hint that the reception was finished.

The President himself accompanied them to the door.

"Hasta luego," he called to them, as they left, and Junior remembered him, waving goodbye with one hand, and still petting the black cat that sat in the crook of his arm.

Pollyanna met her two when they arrived home, with a face full of eager questions waiting to be allowed to pop out.

"Mother, the President is swell! He's just as real and natural and friendly! No swank to him at all. He drank three cups of tea, and talked about the rowing team, and petted his cat. . . ."

"Well," said Jimmy to Pollyanna, as he kissed her, "if the President of Mexico likes me as much as I like him I'll be satisfied."

After she had drunk in everything they could remember to tell her, Pollyanna drew out two packages.

"These came while you were away. One for each of you."

The packages were small, wrapped neatly in white paper, and tied with blue ribbon, over which a seal of wax had been set.

Junior got his open first.

"I got a medal!" he exulted.

Pollyanna said, "Hurry, Jimmy!"

Jimmy drew out a medal too. Both swung from short blue satin ribbons.

"Pollyanna, we're decorated," said Jimmy gravely, pinning his on.

"Here," said Pollyanna, "here's a note in the box yours came in, Jimmy."

The note was simple and direct.

"Somehow I felt that you might like it better if we just talked, and if I sent these to you to look at, and wear, whenever you will," said the note. "Mexico and I appreciate what you have done to advance knowledge of our ancient civilizations and history. This medal is a token of Mexico's and my gratitude."

Jimmy said, "That's from the President, Junior. Put it away and save it. It is a piece of courtesy of genuine intuition and understanding, and it's a letter from a fine man. Save it for both reasons. Some day you'll understand how much to appreciate it."

CHAPTER XXVIII

THE months slipped by. The gold mine was in production now, and Miss Aguamonte was beginning at last to feel her worries lifting, even though her dearest dream —that of being able to bury her father's bones with her mother's in the family plot— was not to be realized.

Ruth was chattering baby Spanish with everyone; even at home, now, her responses to Pollyanna were often in Spanish. This pleased Jimmy endlessly on his trips home.

Junior was frequently with his father at the mine. But now Pollyanna began to think of schools, and the passing of time. She spoke of it to Jimmy one week-end as they sat in the living room before a fire, for it was now too chilly in the patio at night.

"Jimmy, it's only a month away from Christmas. It has been wonderful for the children to get this summer and fall here, to learn Spanish—at least they can understand it and make themselves understood—but what about school? Hadn't we better think about putting them into school here if we are going to stay?"

"Honey, I wasn't going to tell you just yet, but I might as well now. I have just about finished what there is for me to do at the mine. I am going to recommend to Miss Aguamonte that she get a regular man to manage the mine now, and let me go. We could have Christmas in the States. Or here. Wherever you say."

"Jimmy." Pollyanna couldn't make any answer.

"Christmas away from the States will be very different. I love Mexico, and I shall hate to leave. But ... you'll have to be getting a new connection, won't you?"

Pollyanna almost never talked business with Jimmy. She waited to be told his plans, and then she fitted herself into them. She had learned very early in her married life that she would have worries enough running the household and managing the children, without adding Jimmy's professional problems to them. She gave him accounts of her home difficulties after they were settled; he did her the same courtesy with regard to his work.

"I have already had a couple of letters from firms in the States, honey. We might, if you like, close up here, get a car and take the kids with us up north, have Christmas somewhere, and then I'll swing round and look over prospects."

"When would you like to start, Jimmy?" Pollyanna's voice was quiet. The firelight had cast a soft rosy light over her face, and there in the glow of it, with her usual merry expression supplanted for the moment by seriousness. she looked almost sad. Jimmy's love showed i. his eyes as he looked at her. He caught her hand suddenly.

"Sweetheart, if you want to stay, we'll stay."

But Pollyanna's eyes, turned to him immediately, did not say "Stay."

"Dearest, your work is first," she said. "Perhaps we had better go back. We can always come again, can't we? For vacations? It will always seem to be like a little bit of home. That's curious, isn't it? Because we are Anglo-Saxons, and from the very North. Yet here, away from our own sort of surroundings, we have been perfectly content."

"There are two reasons for that, Pollyanna," said Jimmy. "One is the Mexicans themselves, who make everyone feel at home. And one is you, who have the gift of friendship."

* * * * * * *

Pollyanna did not tell the children they were leaving Mexico for a few days.

"I shall have to watch for a good moment in which to tell Judy," she thought, a little worriedly. "The child is going through an emotional stage in her development, and she's so impulsive. I must be careful."

The opportunity seemed to come at the last art class before Christmas holidays. In the general atmosphere of farewells and plans, with Judy putting away her things, and packing them up to carry home, —it seemed a good time.

As they walked along the street, in the bright winter sunshine, Pollyanna said, "Well, Judy dear, that was a real Goodbye you gave your teacher and your friends just now. Daddy says we are to leave Mexico next week."

Judy stood stock still in the street, and her face grew pale.

"Oh, Mother. . . ."

"Won't you like having Christmas in the States, maybe in Hollywood again?"

"I don't want to leave Mexico," said Judy, in a small voice.

"But we'll be coming back again some day," said Pollyanna cheerily, moving Judy along. "We'll all be together, wherever we are. You should be thank-

ful for that. I wonder if you know how many little
girls there are left in schools while their mothers
and fathers travel for pleasure, or because of business. You should be glad that Daddy and I always
take you with us, everywhere."

"I am," whispered Judy, but she was suffering as
only the very young can suffer when their dear-
wrought dream castles topple.

"I have invited the art teacher to tea with us tomorrow, and Jose. I thought we all might go to the
library and see those books once more that you helped
find. It will be a nice thing to remember."

"Yes," said Judy.

* * * * * * *

Junior met his mother at the door with a radiant
face.

"Mother! I've got a surprise for you!"

In the excitement which followed few noticed
Judy's pallor, or her forced answers.

"Here's the surprise, mother. Read the letter!"

He handed her a long white official-looking envelope. The letters danced before Pollyanna's eyes,
but she managed to get the sense of what it said.
Junior had taken second prize in a snapshot contest.

It was his whirling hats—the hats whirling into the bull-ring—which had won the prize. The letter said further that no prize had ever before been granted to a photographer so young. He was congratulated.

"And the prize," shouted Junior, drawing a slip of pink paper out of his pocket, and flourishing it, "is a check for one hundred dollars!"

Pollyanna sat down suddenly.

"Why, Junior! I'm so proud of you!" She kissed him, laughing and crying at once.

"Let me see the check," demanded Ruth. She pored over it, fascinated.

"I suppose now you're photographing everything more madly than ever," said Pollyanna.

"He took pictures of me all afternoon, after the letter came," volunteered Ruth.

Judy brightened suddenly.

"I think that's wonderful, Junior," she said. "I'm proud of you. Would you take a picture of me this afternoon? Now?"

"Sure thing. In the patio. Come on. You too, mother. I want to take pictures of you all, in the patio. Pictures of the house, the cathedral gardens, and everything. To remember it by. Dad says we're going back along the road to San Antonio next week."

"Are we?" asked Ruth.

"Yes, darling. Will you like having your Christmas tree in Hollywood?"

"Will Santa Claus know where we are?"

"Yes, indeed."

"Then I'd like Hollywood," said Ruth.

*   *   *   *   *   *   *

Judy went over to the cathedral to look for Jose, and to tender her mother's invitation.

He was in the belfry, idle, though he had ruled paper and a pencil near by.

"Ah, Judy!" His eyes brightened with pleasure at seeing her.

"Hello, Jose. What are you doing?"

"I was trying to write some music, but I am stupid today. I can't think of anything."

Judy sat down.

"I had my last art class today."

"But you'll be going again, after the holidays, won't you?"

"No. We are going back to the States next week. Dad's work is over here."

She sat very still and looked at her tightly-clenched hands in her lap. She was feeling very sad and very old.

"Then I won't see you any more," said Jose, and his eyes seemed darker than ever, and his boyish face was unhappy.

"Not for a long time," said Judy. "Though of course we will come back some day. And maybe you will come to the States. Who knows?"

"Yes. Quien sabe?"

They sat in silence. Then Judy spoke again.

"Mother wants you to come to tea with us to-morrow. Then we are going to the library, to see those old books from the secret room at Actopan. Remember, I told you about them?"

"Yes."

"Can you come?"

"No, I can't come. Señor Bello has invited some wealthy man to see me and hear me play . . . I am sorry."

"So am I," said Judy blankly. "But of course, I'll come over to say Goodbye again before we leave, anyway."

"I will miss you when you go," said Jose, "and I will never forget you. Sometimes I will write you letters."

"Oh, would you?" A ray of light brightened Judy's small face.

"Yes. You must write first, and tell me where you will be."

"I will."

"You are still my sweetheart. My first sweetheart. I won't have another one, until you tell me that you have forgotten me."

"I will never tell you that," said Judy.

"I wish I could give you a recuerdo, something to remember me by. I cannot yet. But I will send one to you."

"Goodbye Jose."

"No. Hasta luego."

Judy's feet felt light and her heart lighter too, as she skipped down the stone stairs of the belfry.

*   *   *   *   *   *   *

The library room in which the precious old volumes were laid out, under glass cases, for the public to see, was enormously big and light and quiet.

Judy walked about, with her mother and the art teacher, and looked at the volumes, but she found the expedition as a whole disappointing. First of all, Jose could not come. Secondly, these yellowed leaves, with heavy dark writing or printing on them, said little that she could understand. She could not get into the spirit of proprietorship that she had hoped to enjoy, looking at "her discoveries."

Afterward, having tea at the Tacuba café, Polly-

anna commented on her quietness during the hour at
the library.

"Well, they didn't seem like my things," explained
Judy. "Somehow, I almost hoped to find my name
on them! You know?"

"I know," said the art teacher, buttering a bun,
and taking a sip of the glass of rich milk that he
ordered in place of tea.

"But, some day, when you do a piece of work that
is really your own, and can sign your name to it,
you will get a thrill that would never come from any
mere discovery. You are a creative type, anyway
Judy. Your happiness in life will come from making things, and doing things. You will not be like
your mother, who is more genuinely the appreciative
type."

"That's a very good classification of us," agreed
Pollyanna, biting into a sweet cookie, "even though
Judy is so young. What would you advise that I
do to help train her so that she can make the most
of her imagination, her emotional responses, her
quick sensibilities. . . ."

"Well," said the young man, considering, "I don't
think I would encourage them too much. I mean
that. Creative ability does best when it bursts
through bonds and finds its way out impulsively and
impetuously. There are too many slack and senti-

mental and tiresome artists because they have fed
their artistry consciously—they keep remembering
that they are creators, and they forget to live and to
learn discipline."

"I believe you are right," said Pollyanna. "Yet
I was sensitive as a child. I remember my feelings
so well; I have always tried not to outrage those
same feelings in my children. I have tried to be
understanding—a guide and a friend."

"That's all very well for the ordinary child," said
the teacher. "But I believe that the artistic child
must learn self-control, above all things—and while
he learns to appreciate and appraise his own strong
reactions to everything, he must always be thinking
that this excessive power to feel must be met by an
excessive power to regulate and refine.

"For example," said he, pointing to the half-fin-
ished bun on Judy's plate, and her half-drunk cup of
chocolate, "if she had been asked to choose one or
the other, she would have savored the one she chose,
better. And there would have been no waste."

"Well," said Pollyanna, "it is nice to know what
and when to combine too. That is part of discipline.
Part of taste. But you must think about what Señor
Torres just said, Judy. He paid you a high compli-
ment in saying that he thought you had creative talent. In gratitude you must seriously think over what

he has said. You must learn more self-discipline."

Judy's voice rose.

"But I have, I have!" she cried. "I have not cried once about leaving Mexico, but it breaks my heart to go!"

And to the astonishment of Pollyanna and Señor Torres and other late lunchers, she put her head down on her arms and wept bitterly, and aloud.

Pollyanna raised puzzled eyes to Señor Torres. He patted Judy on the shoulder.

"Come, come, dry the tears," he said. "We weren't picking on you. And we want you to be happy. But some day you will learn that hardest lesson of all, too—and that is that we cannot have everything we want, and God sends disappointments to everyone, even the best."

"Poor darling, poor darling," thought Pollyanna, and long after the sobs had ceased, and Judy had dried her eyes, Pollyanna kept saying it inside herself. "The poor silly little darling. . . ."

CHAPTER XXIX

I⊤ was Monday morning, and everyone was busy. Everyone but Ruth. Jimmy was out with Señor Aguilar getting advice on where to buy a new car.

Judy and Pollyanna were making last-minute purchases in town. Lolita was busy with final washing and ironing, for everything was to be packed the next day.

Ruth felt sad to be leaving, in a way. She had friends. There was the black cat in the cathedral gardens, for instance. And Father Mestres. And Lolita. And Jose. And the people in the bakery shop.

She decided to make visits, and say her farewells. The black cat first.

It was a bright day outside, though crisp with the cool air of winter.

A quick search of the cathedral gardens revealed nothing, and Ruth's spirits sagged. She wanted so much to sit and pet the black cat, and measure the long white whiskers against her short fat fingers.

310

Round and round the garden she plodded, looking
more carefully. No success.

A little breeze had sprung up, and the cool clouds
were racing across the shining sky. She would feel
cold if she stayed longer in the garden.

The bells had begun to sound, very loud and close
above her. She brightened. At least she would find
Jose and his father in. That would be something.
She began, painfully, to climb the steep stone steps,
with the clangor of the bells growing louder in her
ears every minute. But she wearied very soon, and
to rest herself, and also to see what lay inside that
little door that led into somewhere from the belfry
steps, she decided this time to push it open and go in.

The little door let her into a balcony overhanging
the main hall of the church. It was warm and dark
up here in the loft, and the jeweled-light from the
colored windows above fell down in squares of
amethyst, topaz, sapphire, and emerald on the little
girl's apron, and on her small round face, and on
her hands, like two little starfishes.

Ruth looked down into the great church. There
were one or two people in there, on their knees, silently praying, their rosaries slipping round in their
fingers gently. Candles were burning at the altar,
and little votive lights twinkled warmly inside red
glass.

Suddenly she felt something soft against her ankle. Frightened, she looked down, into two glowing eyes. But she stifled the cry that rose to her lips, as she heard a faint "Me-ow."

She knelt down, and felt about. It was the black cat. And with her were four tiny balls of wettish wool. Four tiny kittens. Ruth's heart almost broke with tenderness and pleasure. That she should be the one to find the black cat's kittens! It was wonderful. Other little girls had found kittens, or puppies, but never Ruth. Now these were her very own. Finders keepers.

She put trembling fingers on the little warm things. The black mother cat nuzzled her worriedly.

"If I could put them all in my apron, I could take them home," thought Ruth, but she knew that she could not take the four kittens and the mother cat all in her apron. And it would worry the black cat to take away her kittens. What to do?

Jose. He would know.

She crept quietly out of the little balcony loft, and began to toil up the stairs again, thinking that if Jose could bring the mother cat, she could bring the kittens, and then. . . .

But the awful importance of time flashed into her mind, and at the thoughts that came with it, her heart failed her, and she opened her mouth and wept aloud, and the tears fell fast as rain down her cheeks.

Because of her wails, Jose met her at the top of the stairs, worried.

"What is the matter, chulita? Ruthie, always you are crying? Have you no happiness in your heart?"

"Oh Jose," she moaned, flinging herself into his arms. "We're going away day after tomorrow, and I've found kittens. I guess they won't let me take them with me. My first kittens too. Oh, I want them."

Jose was wearing a heavy sweater. The glow of his little brazier of coals showed from underneath one of the closed doors. In winter it was too cold to use the mirador.

Into that glowing small room Jose led her. His father was already lying down on a couch, with warm robes over him. From the little brazier came a fan-like warmth.

"Now, warm those cold hands," said Jose. "Where are those kittens you have found?"

"You know that little door, half way down, that's usually closed?"

"Yes."

"Well, today it was a little bit open, and I went in. And there was the black cat, with four little tiny kittens."

"Let's go see. Will you be all right, Father? Warm enough?"

The man nodded gratefully without speaking.

Ruth and Jose went down the stairs.

The black cat was still there with her kittens. Jose lifted one and looked at its tiny pink mouth, little soft weak pink paws, and screwed-up little face, with small dabs of ears and closed eyes.

"You could never take these with you, Ruth. They're too tiny. They need their mother."

"I know it." The tears fell again. "I hate to go without them," she gasped out. "My first kittens."

"I'll tell you," said Jose. "I'll keep them for you. I'll look after them well, and I'll send you pictures of them."

"Oh, will you?"

"Yes, I promise."

Ruth dried her tears. She lifted each tiny kitten and kissed it solemnly.

"Goodbye," she said to each.

Then, "Goodbye, Jose," she said. "Don't forget to write."

"I won't."

Ruth descended the stairs.

* * * * * * *

Father Mestres was in the garden. He smiled gladly as he saw Ruth coming. He laid a kind finger against her cheek, still wet with the tears she had shed at parting with the kittens.

"Little girls cry so much," he said softly, as if to himself. "Little girls, and big ones, too. Yet the world is so full—so much sun, so much to enjoy, God and his love all around, everywhere. Yet the tears fall, always."

"Mama never cries," said Ruth, taking his hand, and walking with him through the garden. Father Mestres stopped many times to pinch off a dying bloom that marred the beauty of some bush.

"Your mother holds in her heart the secret of happiness," he said. "To her, all things have in them their measure of good and of joy. All things come from God, everything that happens is part of God's will. We are all his creatures. We should never cry."

"No," agreed Ruth, but in such a doleful voice, that Father Mestres stopped and laughed aloud.

"I hate to go away," said Ruth. "I hate to say 'Goodbye.' "

"We won't say Goodbye then," said Father Mestres serenely. "We'll say, 'Hasta luego,' which means, 'Till we meet again.' "

"Does it mean we really will meet again?"

"Yes, almost that."

"I found some kittens up there in the church," said Ruth. "The black cat has them. I cried because I wanted to take them with me, but Jose says he will take care of them for me."

"When you come back, your kittens will be big cats," said Father Mestres. "Big and healthy. They'll have their eyes open, and they'll be able to get acquainted with you, be your friend. Little tiny kittens can't even open their eyes for a while, you know. You could love them, but they wouldn't love you."

Hand in hand, walking, they talked. And when at last they parted, Father Mestres blessed the little girl, and made over her the sign of his faith.

Ruth herself was never to forget that last quiet afternoon in the cathedral gardens, talking to Father Mestres. Later in her life, with that seeming irrelevance that attends so many of our sudden memories, she was to be there in that Mexican garden many times when she had need of comfort.

The people in the bakery shop were glad to see her. They were incredulous that she must say Goodbye. Really going away? Forever? Oh no, not forever. And they kissed her, the baker and his wife, and cuddled her, and gave her too many sugary cookies. There were crumbs on her chin, and sugar made her fingers sticky when she got home. It was almost dark. Lolita, in her savory kitchen, was fussing over a package.

"Where have you been so long, Queridita?"

"I was telling everyone Goodbye. You're last, Lolita. But one of the best."

Ruth felt sad again. She clutched Lolita's apron and hid her face.

"Probrecita, queridita," crooned Lolita, picking her up, and swaying with her in her arms. "I have made you a big package of dulces—candies. You can eat them on the way. You won't forget Lolita? You'll come back again to Mexico?"

"Yes," said Ruth. "I'll come back. I'll come back as soon as my kittens are big. In a year, anyway. Mama will bring me back."

"Yes, yes, of course she will."

But Lolita's eyes shone with tears too.

CHAPTER XXX

HASTA LUEGO

PACKED and ready and starting. All farewells
had been said. All loving messages had been received. Addresses had been written down. Prom-
ises to write had been given. Baggage had been
shipped. The door of the little pink house by the
cathedral had closed behind them, and the bells of
the church grew fainter in their ears as they rolled
away down the street.

It was early morning. There was a freshness in
the air, a new-washed cleanliness about the sunlight
that lay over the iron-barred small houses like gold,
a brilliance to the purple-red clumps of bougainvillea
that tumbled over fences and house-tops.

They came into Mexico City. Past the Geneve
Hotel, from which a gay party of tourists were already starting out, loaded with cameras, guides,
packages of luncheon and umbrellas. Down along
Chapultepec Avenue, where a bit of old Aqueduct
still stood, painted a lovely color by time, and on
which grew wild flowers; past the statues in the

318

center of the broad avenue, past all the lovely dignified homes of the wealthy in the capital city. Past
the great new theatre, built of marble, so heavy that
it sank below the level of the sidewalk. Past the
cathedral and the governor's palace.

Pollyanna rode in back with Ruth and Judy.
Jimmy was driving the new car, and Junior, with his
camera slung over his shoulder on straps, was beside him.

"No," said Jimmy, a little impatiently, "we are not
going to stop every two minutes and let you get out
and tinker with your camera for hours getting proper
lights and distances and focusing. You have won
enough honors with that machine for now. Forget it
for a while."

"Be glad," called Pollyanna from the back seat,
"that you are left with a legitimate excuse to come
back, Junior!"

"Well, as to that," said Jimmy, "I don't think any
of us will need legitimate excuses. We won't need
any excuse. We'll all just come."

Judy's heart felt heavy as a stone inside her. She
thought, "I shall never be happy again."

But, as a matter of fact, she was singing before they
had sped along the blue ribbon of road past Pachuca,
and had begun to tell Ruth the legend of Los Frailes.

It was two days before they came into the glossy-

green orange-growing country, for they took their
time, lingering over lovely views, gathering flowers,
enjoying this last trip along the road from Mexico
City, as people take their dessert slowly, sorry to end
the gustatory and conversational delights of a meal.

From the mountains Pollyanna and the children
got again the intense delight that had been theirs
on the drive down.   They often spoke of Señor
Moreno.

"Will we stay long in Monterey, Daddy?"

"Probably two days," said Jimmy.   "I have business with Miss Aguamonte.   You'll enjoy your two
days though.   You can take some trips.   You can see
Chipinque, and the Horse-Tail Falls, and you can
see the soccer games."

"I remember Monterey," said Judy.   "I liked it.
I'm glad we're going to stay."

* * * * * * *

Down, down out of the mountains, and they came
into Saltillo, under a clear high bright blue sky.
They had been on the road four days, though if
Jimmy had wanted to drive faster, he could have been
there two days ago.

"And in a few hours we'll be in Monterey," said
Pollyanna.

The road ran along through dryish country, where

maguey bushes and little clumps of greasewood grew
alternating with green-leaved tall trees that seemed
to tremble in the sun.

"I see it, I see it!" screamed Ruth, after an hour.

"What?"

"Monterey. There's the Saddle Mountain!"

"Yes, here we are. And we are almost out of
Mexico now. From here the road stretches straight
into Texas—only three hours away."

"Well, it may be near the States, but it is still
Mexico," said Pollyanna, as the car slid into the
narrow streets of the town, and again, as they rode,
they looked into barred-windowed rooms, and caught
fleeting glimpses of bright patios.

They were royally welcomed at the Hotel, and
when they saw Miss Aguamonte later, for dinner,
they found in place of the constrained, sad-faced
woman they had met before, a happy-eyed lady,
bubbling with plans for herself and her sister, whose
illness had taken a turn for the better. She still wore
a white dress, and the black cross against her throat,
but that cross bounced frequently as her laughter
bubbled up, and her eyes sparkled.

"I can never thank you enough, Señor Pendleton, for all you have done for me. You were very
brave, and you have been very generous to me. As
a token of my appreciation, will you permit me to

give Mrs. Pendleton a small remembrance, of me, and of Mexico?"

"I'm delighted," said Jimmy.

"And I'm enchanted!" cried Pollyanna, as she tried on her own wrist the bracelet of Queretaro opals that Miss Aguamonte had unlocked off her own, and placed in her hand.

"They say that opals are bad luck if they are not given by a friend," said Miss Aguamonte. "But the gratitude and esteem that goes with this gift, should make it into a good luck piece!"

"I'm sure of it," said Pollyanna.

The stones glowed blue and red and orange and fiery dark blue like flame.

"And these stones will bring you back some day, for the opals of Mexico always long for home," said Miss Aguamonte. "And that is why I give them to you. You must come back."

"I know that we will," said Pollyanna.

And two days later, when the road that had brought them from Mexico City, through loveliness and age-old wonders to Monterey, approached the border, Pollyanna turned and looked back into Mexico.

"Hasta luego," she whispered, for she would not say Goodbye.

THE END